SHADOW & ASH

BLOODBOUND

Timoteu Montroig

Prologue

It was the onset of winter and the shop was bustling with activity as the customers rummaged for supplies before the first snowstorm of the season. The climate of the region was harsh and unforgiving and many of the residents of the outlying villages generally ended up being snowed in for months at a time.

I glanced around the shelves stocked with produce and spied a stack of burlap sacks containing rice. I grabbed one from the top of the pile, heft it onto my shoulder and began to weave my way through the throng of people to the storekeeper. Casually dropping the bag onto the floor at my feet, I made eye contact and smiled.

"Back so soon?" the burly man said, clapping his hand on my shoulder in a friendly gesture. He was about sixty years old, bald and wearing a long colorful robe that hung to his feet.

"I was halfway out of town before I remembered I needed rice!" I replied.

I had known the jovial man my entire life. Of all the places I visited on the numerous supply runs into town with my father, this was my favorite. The owner's wife had taken a liking to me and I rarely left empty-handed—invariably exiting with some freshly made sweet bread clutched in my tiny palm! I think she considered me a little malnourished since she would frequently chastise my father.

"Have you been feeding the lad?" she would tease. "We need to put some meat on his bones!"

"This boy could eat my horse and not gain a single ounce in weight," he would laugh back.

The warmth of the shop felt comforting amidst the cold, a refuge where villagers lingered to swap stories and enjoy the simple pleasure of a friendly face. The air inside was a mixture of scents: dried herbs hanging from the beams, fresh loaves cooling on a wooden rack, and the faint sweetness of spices from the far corner. For a moment, I was reluctant to step back outside into the biting air, but it was time to get home and I preferred not to travel at night.

With a final wave to the storekeeper, I walked out onto the busy street—lined with market stalls, all of which were brimming with goods. It was the largest market for miles and one could purchase just about anything from fabric, pots, farming tools, weapons, to meat and vegetables.

My cart was standing next to the neighboring shop and fully laden with supplies, all of which were covered by a multi-colored quilt of animal hides secured by a coarse rope. I made my way to the back and lifted a portion of the covering, adding the sack of rice to its load. It was then I noticed a tall man with shoulder length grey hair and an outstretched palm. He was holding an apple just under the nose of my horse, caressing its mane with his free hand and speaking softly into its ear.

"This is a beautiful beast," he remarked, without so much as a glance in my direction.

"Thank you," I replied.

My horse finished exploring the apple with its nose, opened its mouth and in a few swift bites it was gone.

After a brief pause and in a tone of voice that almost sounded accusatory, he added. "It's a shame to see such a magnificent animal pulling a cart!" His head was gently shaking from side to side while he spoke.

The man was beginning to irritate me. He did not know anything about my life and was already making judgments about my choice to use the horse to pull my cart. I sucked in a breath and tried to remain polite.

"I know, but I don't have much choice in the matter. My carthorse died a few months ago."

Now I was making excuses and attempting to explain myself to him, a complete stranger. This just served to heighten my growing irritation.

The man simply grunted and continued to stroke the beast's mane. With his attention diverted, I took the opportunity to study him more intently. From what I could tell he appeared to be around fifty years of age. His skin was extremely pale in comparison to the dark olive that was common for the region. He was well dressed for a traveler, but practically so. Everything he wore was specifically tailored for a person who spent a lot of time on the road. Strapped to his back were two curved swords, their pommels extending above his shoulders.

Given my brief assessment of him, there was little doubt in my mind that this man knew how to fight. There was something about him, a poise, gracefulness and efficiency of movement. It was also rare to see someone in possession of two such weapons. It took years of practice to master one and only the greatest of sword master adepts would be able to handle two.

"It's military bred?" he questioned. The statement sounded more rhetorical than an actual question, so I stayed silent.

"Whence did you come by it?"

"My father, he was an officer in the army."

"Ah," he replied, nodding in understanding.

Tiring from the interaction I hauled myself onto the seat of the cart. It was about 15 leagues to the little wooded valley where I lived and I wanted to make it back before dark.

"Thanks for the apple, but I need to head off."

The stranger glanced in my direction and I met his eyes. They were deep blue, piercing and displayed a keen intelligence. I felt a rising unease in my chest. The man gave off an air that was almost predatory and my desire to depart became more urgent.

It came with a sense of relief when he simply responded with a curt nod—his lips turning up with a hint of a smile.

"Safe travels."

He then turned on his heals and walked briskly into the crowd.

I gave the reins a brief shake. The cart lurched into motion and I began the long trek home. Glancing back, the stranger was nowhere in sight.

~

The sun was only partly visible as it gradually ebbed below the crest of the mountain that bordered the forest where I lived. It was dusk and I was anticipating the moment I could put my feet up next to the hearth with a bowl of stew and some bread. It had been a long day and I was famished.

Lost in thought, I rounded a bend in the trail. The tall trees on either side were now completely masking the sun from view and it was becoming difficult to see.

It was then that I noticed the dark shape obstructing my path, something akin to a small log. Tugging on the reins, my cart came to a standstill and I stood up for a better view. Whatever the shape was, it was partially hidden from view by the head of my horse.

I hopped down and made my way down the road. The nature of the obstruction soon became apparent. Directly in front of me was the body of a man wearing a dirty beige colored *chiton.* It was made of linen, filled with holes and what was left of it covered the majority of the prone body from just above the knees. There was a simple brown leather belt strapped around his waist and attached to it was an empty scabbard. I guessed that it had once held a short hunting knife.

I groaned. It looked like the man had been robbed and left for dead. In fact, he probably was dead and it unnerved me that there may be bandits close to where I lived.

I knelt and as my father had taught me, and felt for the man's pulse. No sooner than my fingers came into contact with his neck, I was startled by a loud snap of a twig. I turned. My eyes came to rest on four men dressed in similar attire to the body, standing strategically between where I was kneeling and my horse.

"Hey lads, look what we have here!" one of them said as he flexed his fingers. He then gently rested his right hand on the pommel of the sword that was in a scabbard tied to his waist. The brigand had long unkempt curly black hair and an intricate tattoo that covered half his face. He was the epitome of what you would consider a bandit, just like the ones described in the stories I was told as a child.

The entire group burst into laughter and began to walk forward drawing their swords.

I glanced beyond them to the seat of my cart where my own sword lay. Feeling a sense of panic, I realized that I was out of options. There was no way I could get to my weapon and all I had on me was a small hunting knife. Even if I could have made it to my sword, it would not have mattered. I was heavily outnumbered. There would be little chance that I could take them all on at once.

As I considered the limited choices available to me, I was shocked to feel the sharp point of a knife. It had pierced my tunic and was pressed against the center of my back. I froze and the blood drained from my face.

"Don't move," a voice growled.

The man I thought was dead was actually very much alive. He had simply been the bait and I had, like an idiot, fallen right into their trap. In my desire to get home I had been careless and was now paying the price, one that would probably cost me my life!

I gradually raised my hands with my palms open.

"I don't want any trouble. Please, just take what you need."

"Oh, we intend to," said the man with the tattoo, who was obviously their leader. After a moment of deliberation, he added, "Kill him!"

"Wait!" I screamed. "I have silver—at my home—I can show you where I've hidden it!"

My pulse was racing and I was frantically trying to buy some time. I needed to stay alive long enough to create an opening, one that would involve me reaching my sword. I would rather go down fighting than have my throat slit like a pig at harvest festival.

The tattooed man paused and looked at me critically, clearly deliberating his next move.

"If you're lying, you'll wish for the quick death I was about to give you. I'll take pleasure in making it long and painful. You'll end up begging me to kill you!"

A hand grabbed my arm from behind and roughly pulled me to my feet. I was then disarmed and shoved toward the cart.

"Find some rope and bind him. We can't have our prey running off now, can we?"

A few minutes later, with my wrists bound behind my back, I was leading the group of bandits unceremoniously toward my home.

~

It was now completely dark and we were about a mile away from where I lived. The coming of night had worked in my favor and I had spent the last hour working on the rope that bound my wrist. Under the cover of darkness none of the men had noticed and with a final pull, my hands slipped free. I kept them behind my back and prayed that I had not been seen.

I waited for my opportunity. On the fringe of the forest that surrounded my hut was a fallen tree. I had felled it the day before and the long-handled axe was still lodged in its trunk.

As the road widened into a clearing and the silhouette of my hut came into view, I made my move. I brought my hands out from behind my back and shoved the man to my right with such force that he stumbled and fell. Sprinting, I made for the tree line off to my right. I could hear the men shouting behind me.

The leader's voice rang out above the rest as he screamed, "Get the son of a whore!"

It was dark, but I was finally on land I was inherently familiar with. It was the opening I had been waiting for, one that would help even the odds.

I leapt over a small brook and with a sense of satisfaction heard the man closest to me curse as he lost his footing and fell into it with a loud splash.

Reaching the fallen tree, I pulled the axe free and turned just in time to block the swing of a sword whose tip would have sliced open my throat. The blade rang as it struck the handle of the axe. Holding it with both hands, about three feet apart, I was using it as a makeshift shield.

Before the man could take another swing, I lashed out with my foot and caught him in the groin. Screaming in pain he doubled over. I then brought my hands together at the end of the handle, simultaneously dropping my head, pivoting and bringing the full force of my axe to bear on the next man to reach me. It was fortunate that my instincts had told me to duck since his sword narrowly missed the top of my head. I stepped forward inside the man's guard just as my axe completed its swing. There was a dull thud and he dropped his sword. The man looked down in horror at his eviscerated stomach and collapsed to his knees, coughing up blood as he did so.

The remaining four men now had me surrounded and they were warily circling me. Regrettably, the one I had kicked in the groin was standing at full height again. It was obvious from the way he was looking at me that he was not happy.

"Drop your axe, show us where the silver is and I may consider letting you live," the leader said.

"I'm not an idiot," I replied through gritted teeth.

"Have it your way!"

The men closed in and I swung the axe in a wide arc. It struck a sword, knocking it from the hand of one of the bandits. However, I was not quick enough to stop the thrust from behind. There was a sharp sensation of pain as a sword penetrated me. Glancing down I discovered its tip protruding from the center of my chest.

The man pulled his sword free and stepped away. My legs gave way and I slowly collapsed, falling onto my back. Gazing up at the four faces that now encircled me I had no choice but to accept and make peace with the fact that my life was over.

"You had to make this hard," the tattooed leader sneered. "Leave him, let's go search the—."

The sentence was abruptly cut off as his head fell from his shoulders and landed between my legs. He remained standing for a few seconds with blood fountaining from his severed neck and then crumpled to the ground.

The three remaining men pivoted on their heels, swords poised.

"What the—," one of them exclaimed. However, just like the tattooed leader, he never finished. Instead, a gurgling sound emitted from his mouth. He dropped his sword and clutched at his throat. Blood was pouring from between his fingers as he rotated towards me and collapsed.

Everything then happened in a matter of heartbeats. A dark form closed in at an inhuman speed, so fast that I could barely follow its movements. It passed over me in the blink of an eye, severing the sword hand of one bandit and then decapitating the other. Coming to a standstill, it eyed the man who was now screaming and clutching his handless stump. The figure then casually strolled over to him and, with a single efficient swing, decapitated him. The head fell to the ground and rolled, coming to a stop right next to the head of the man who had been their leader. The tattooed face was facing me, his vacant eyes staring into mine.

The dark form, now silhouetted by the moon, made his way over to me. I could no longer feel my legs and was unable to move. He knelt and pulled back the hood of his dark cloak. I felt a wave of recognition. I was staring into the eyes of the man I had met at the market.

"You are dying," he said in a tone of voice that almost seemed sympathetic.

“I know,” I sputtered in reply.

"I saw them trailing your wagon and then slip unseen into the forest ahead of you. Normally, I don't like to interfere, but my conscience eventually got the better of me. If I had acted sooner, this could have been prevented. I apologize for the delay."

I could just make out the lines of his forehead as they furrowed. He seemed to be deliberating. After a moment's hesitation he added, “We don’t have much time. I may be able to save your life, but the odds are not in your favor. What I’m proposing may kill you, but there is a small chance that you will survive”

I laughed, coughing up blood and then swallowed in an attempt to find my breath. “I’ve got nothing to lose. I’m dead either way.”

“So—do I have your permission to try?” he questioned.

“Yes,” I whispered faintly.

My vision was growing dark but I could still make out his face as it descended toward me. There was a sharp pain in my neck followed by numbness and a sense of euphoria. My lips curled into a smile and everything went black.

Chapter One

Aristion

490 BCE

Lying on my stomach at the top of the cliffs I gazed out at the placid blue waters of what the Persian's called the *Darya-ye Mazandaran.*

It was midday and the sun was at its zenith. The humidity was almost unbearable and my shirt and pants were now plastered to my skin. The fact that my disguise also included a knee length kaftan and turban only served to exacerbate the situation. How I longed to strip naked and dive into the cool water.

It was the perfect hiding place. The trees were dense and also provided a degree of relief from the sun. I had been there a few hours and was assessing the size of the fleet that was sprawled across the bay below me.

The galleys had been gathering over the course of the past week. My final count put their number close to 600. They were quite a sight to behold. Long and sleek, with curved bows that looked like a crescent moons. Each had a single mast and a row of oars, all of which had been retracted.

I had spent many years studying all aspects of warfare and the number of ships did not bode well for the Greeks. Each could carry 32-34 soldiers. I therefore estimated the potential size of the army to be around 20,000 men. This was confirmed by the sea of tents located on the flat area of ground just to the south of my current hiding place. They stretched as far as the eye could see and the camp was teaming with activity.

It was time to go. I had a long ride ahead of me and it was urgent that I relay the news of the Persian fleet to the Spartan's and the Athenian general, Miltiades. If they did not have time to prepare for the coming invasion, all would be lost.

I turned and crawled away from the edge of the cliff. Once obscured by the densely packed vegetation I got to my feet and made my way toward the clearing where I had left my stallion.

It was not far and within a few minutes my horse came into view—along with six men. They were gathered with their backs to me. All were garbed in Sasanian dress, riding attire consisting of loose-fitting trousers, boots, and knee-length tunics bound with a leather belt. Strapped to their waists were *shamshirs*, long curved Persian swords; similar to the one I was carrying. I liked the name *shamshir* since it felt aptly appropriate. Translated it stood for *Lions fang.*

I hesitated and then, after a brief moment of deliberation, walked into the glade.

"Greetings, can I help you?" I said with a smile, speaking in Farsi, their native tongue.

Surprised by my silent entrance they spun to face me, hands dropping to the hilts of their swords.

"Easy, easy … I don't want any trouble!"

"Who are you? What are you doing here?" one of them shouted.

Still smiling, I took stock of the man who had spoken—my gaze eventually coming to rest on his sword. The pommel of the weapon was protruding beyond his clenched fist and I could clearly make out a crescent moon and dagger etched into the silver.

I froze.

The smile left my face.

Raising my eyes to meet his I simply hissed one word, "*Shikari!*"—the Farsi word for hunter.

Any desire to talk my way out of the situation had evaporated the moment my eyes had come to rest on the symbol. These men were going to die.

Everything seemed to slow as I sprang into action. The men's faces registered surprise as I closed the distance with a speed that, to any bystander, would have seemed impossible.

The first man fell before he had even fully drawn his sword, a fountain of blood spouting from the opening my weapon had made across his throat. Slipping by him, I instinctively ducked, spinning on the balls of my feet as I did so. My sword completed its second circle and made contact, severing the spine of the man to his left just as a blade passed over my head. Somersaulting backward, one hand touching the ground, I landed on both feet in a crouch.

As I straightened, the two men I had struck collapsed to the ground and I leveled my gaze upon the remaining four. They had recovered from the shock of my brutal attack and were now facing me, swords at the ready.

"*Galla!*" one of them spat.

I smiled.

It was the Persian word for demon.

The men were Zoroastrian Warrior Clerics, members of an elite order of assassins that had been established by Darius the Great, the third King of Kings of the Achaemenid dynasty of Persia.

Darius was a devout follower of the Zoroastrianistic faith, a religion that embraced a dualistic cosmology of good versus evil.

Unlike the Greek's, who believed in many God's, the major precept of Zoroastrianism was the existence a single supreme being, a benevolent deity of wisdom, *Ahura Mazda* or Wise Lord.

Darius subscribed to the eschatology that predicted the ultimate conquest of good over evil and many of his actions were driven by his desire to bring this event into actuality.

The Zoroastrian Warrior Clerics were both judge and executioner. Operating under the direct orders of Darius, they actively sought out what they perceived as evil, in all its shapes and forms, and eradicated it.

The four clerics still on their feet, eyed me apprehensively. As well trained as they were, they were no match for someone such as me. They lacked sufficient warriors, and there did not appear to be a *mágos* in their company. Typically, it took at least twenty of their order, working in unison with a *mágos*—a practitioner of magic—to incapacitate a single vrykolakas, the name we had given our kind.

"Even if you succeed in killing us, more will follow. We won't stop until your taint is cleansed from this world!" one of them shouted. His voice trembled, betraying the fear he tried to mask. He gripped the pommel of his *shamshir* so tightly that his knuckles had turned white. Terror flickered in his eyes, and the veins in his neck pulsed with the frantic rhythm of his heartbeat.

I advanced, then broke into a sprint. My body became a blur of motion, moving with supernatural speed. Time seemed to slow, and my enemies' movements appeared sluggish, as if they were fighting underwater. Their attacks were telegraphed and easy to anticipate. I effortlessly sidestepped and dodged their thrusts, weaving through them with precision. Each step was deliberate, my senses heightened, capturing every detail—the flicker of fear in their eyes, the sweat on their brows, the quiver in their hands. The sound of their labored breathing and the clank of their weapons filled the air, but I was already several moves ahead, executing my attacks with unerring accuracy.

Moving between the two on my left, spinning as I did so, my sword cleanly removed the head of one and sliced open the throat of the other. I then parried a thrust from a third, stepped inside his guard, and brought the top of my head down hard on the bridge of his nose. As he staggered back, I impaled him with my sword. Glancing at the final combatant, still unscathed, I saw him attempting to circle behind me. The moment our eyes locked, he froze, the color draining from his face. Realizing his death was imminent, his shoulders slumped in defeat.

"Please—please—spare me," he screamed, dropping his sword.

"You won't get any mercy from me. Darius declared war on my kind, a mistake both you and he will pay for with your lives," I replied, my voice dripping with disgust.

I began to walk toward him, each step deliberate and measured.

With a yelp, he turned on his heels and bolted. He didn't get far. Terror clouded his vision, causing his feet to become snagged on a fallen tree branch. He stumbled and landed headfirst in the dirt. Before he could regain his footing, I was upon him.

Straddling his back, I bit down, my extended incisors piercing the bulging vein on the left side of his neck.

I had not taken blood for days, and it felt good to feed. A surge of strength and vitality flowed through me, an intoxicating rush that invigorated every cell in my body. The warm, metallic taste filled my mouth, driving away the fatigue that had been weighing me down. My muscles, once heavy with exhaustion, now felt lithe and powerful and the world around me suddenly became brighter and more vivid.

It didn't take long. His initial writhing gradually slowed, and soon the body beneath me went limp, lapsing into unconsciousness. The forest around us grew still, the only sounds the faint rustling of leaves and the steady rhythm of his fading heartbeat.

Satiated, I sat back on my heals and gazed down as the blood continued to pour from the open punctures I had left on his neck. I had the ability to heal the wound, but this man was a killer and did not deserve to live.

Rising to my feet I looked down one last time, just as the man gave a final exhale and passed from this world into the next.

Chapter Two

Kallian

490 BCE

Kallian leaned back just as a sword tip narrowly missed his chest. Instantaneously, he pivoted slightly to his left and brought his own sword up, blocking a second swing that was coming at him in a downward arc. The weapons clashed and the noise of their impact reverberated off the surrounding buildings.

Dropping into a crouch, Kallian lashed out with his foot in a sweeping motion, causing his opponent to jump back. Narrowly missing the man's shin, he then summersaulted backwards to put some distance between them.

The two combatants were now a few feet apart and began to circle each other looking for an opening. Beads of sweat were dripping down his face and he casually swept the hair out of his eyes with the back of his hand.

"You have improved," the older boy stated with a grin.

Kallian was fourteen years old and his bronze body was lean and athletic from many years of training. He had curly black hair that fell to his shoulders, one of which had a scar from a sword cut. However, of all his features, his eyes were the most striking. They were a deep shade of blue and shone with an intense luminosity.

His mother had named him Kallian, which meant "most beautiful". She had died a few days after his first birthday and he had no memory of her. Raised by his aunt, he had spent his early years living on the banks of the Eurotas River, just south of the capital city of Sparta.

At the age of seven, as with the majority of Spartan boys, Kallian was assigned to a military training camp called an *agōgē*.

Life at the *agōgē* was hard. Its sole purpose was to turn young men into warriors. As part of their training, Kallian and the other boys were intentionally underfed and encouraged to steal food. There was one proviso. Don't get caught! He had learnt this the hard way and had been mercilessly whipped for his failure. He vowed to never let it happen again and soon became adept at pilfering what he required. On one occasion he had even managed to steal a knife from his commanding officer's dinner plate. The man had turned his back to address a messenger and Kallian, seeing the opportunity, had taken it without a second thought.

The other boys had been rough on him, especially during the first three years. He had been beaten so many times that he lost count. However, rather than demoralizing him, it had served to motivate him—to become better, stronger, and faster. There had been many evenings when he spent endless hours training in private while the other boys relaxed and told stories by the fire.

Eventually, Kallian's dedication finally paid off. By the time he was fourteen he was best fighter in his *agélai*, the group of boys he had been assigned to when he joined the *agōgē*.

~

Kallian's opponent, Eioneus, was four years older and extremely proficient with a sword. After ten minutes of sparring, Kallian had yet to land a blow. The arena, a circular pit surrounded by stone seats, echoed with the sounds of clashing metal and the murmurs of an intrigued audience.

Kallian rushed at Eioneus. He dipped and weaved left as he slashed downward. Eioneus parried, the blades shrieking, metal against metal, sparks flying into the air. The sun caught the edges of their swords, creating dazzling flashes of light. Eioneus then sidestepped to the right just as Kallian's next swing passed a hair's breadth from his face, the force of the miss causing a rush of air to brush Eioneus's cheek.

Finally, with the speed of a viper, Eioneus punched him in the solar plexus, causing him to double over, before ending the fight with a swift uppercut—striking Kallian directly under the chin. The crowd watching the fight let out a collective wince as Kallian flew backward, landing on the ground with an audible thud that reverberated through the arena.

Eioneus walked toward Kallian, his bronze torso glistening as the sunlight struck the moisture on his body. His long black hair, damp with sweat, clung to his shoulders, and his lean muscles, still taut from the exertion, rippled with each step. He was a sight to behold, naked as the day he was born, save for his sword. He reminded Kallian of the statue of Apollo that stood in the central square, every inch a god of strength and beauty.

He reached down and grasped Kallian's forearm, pulling him to his feet with effortless strength.

"You put up a good fight, little brother," he laughed, his voice rich and warm, resonating with genuine affection and pride.

"Not good enough it appears," Kallian replied, wincing from the pain of the blow he had received to his stomach.

The bystanders had started to disperse and the two boys were now alone.

"Let's go grab some food. I'm famished!"

"I'll join you in a few minutes. I need to cool off. The river is calling me!"

Eioneus thought for a second and then slapped Kallian on the back, "That sounds like a great idea, I'll join you. We can eat after."

The two of them made their way out of the arena and, within a few minutes, found themselves standing on a small outcropping of rock. The landscape stretched out before them, a breathtaking panorama of lush greenery and rolling hills. Below, the Eurotas River glistened in the sunlight, its clear, cool waters sparkling invitingly. The gentle sound of the flowing river, combined with the rustling leaves of nearby trees, created a sense of tranquility, a stark contrast to the intensity of the arena.

They carefully placed their swords on the ground, the metal glinting in the sunlight, walked to the edge of the rock and gazed at the pristine river below. With a shared look, they plunged naked into the refreshing embrace of the Eurotas, the cool water invigorating their senses as it washed away the sweat and grime of the arena.

Chapter Three

Aristion

490 BCE

I was 32 years of age when I died and was born into my new life. Over 70 years had now passed and I did not look a day older.

I still remember the day of my turning as clearly as if it had happened yesterday. Lying by the trunk of a tree, I'd regained consciousness and opened my eyes. Vision blurred; it had taken a few minutes for my surroundings to come into focus. Where was I? What had happened? My thoughts were jumbled and I felt an intense feeling of disorientation.

"Welcome back!"

Seeking the source of the greeting, my eyes came to rest on the stranger I'd met at the market. He was crouching next to me, resting on his heals.

"You are lucky to be alive."

It all came flooding back. The bandits, my attempt to flee, the fight and finally the sword thrust through my chest.

I pushed myself up to a sitting position, with my back to the tree and explored the location of the wound with my hand. To my surprise there was nothing to be found! This couldn't be. How was it even possible? Frantically, I began to explore my entire body. Still nothing, not even a scratch. There was blood on my clothing and it had been punctured, but that was it.

"What did you do? I should be dead!" I exclaimed.

"You were," the stranger smiled.

"No—this can't be possible."

"I assure you it is."

"How?"

"I turned you."

"Turned?"

"You are like me now—a vrykolakas."

I froze, and the blood drained from my face. No, this could not be. Vrykolakas were the stuff of fairy tales, the stories parents told their children to keep them in line. It was quite common for a child to be chastised with, "You know what happens if you misbehave—a vrykolakas will sneak into your room at night and eat you!" Yet, as I sat with my back against the tree, the terror of those childhood warnings now felt all too real. The thought of those mythic creatures existing beyond the realm of bedtime stories sent a chill down my spine. How could the legends be true?

I closed my eyes in an attempt to process what he was telling me.

"You don't know how lucky you are. Only one out of fifty survive a turning. It's rare for any to attempt it."

He paused and eyed me speculatively before continuing, his voice softer.

"If I hadn't acted, we would not be having this conversation right now. You wouldn't have made it. Truly, there was little to lose."

This was a lot to handle and I took a deep breath, resting my head back against the trunk of the tree. The stranger, still squatting, eyed me quizzically.

"Who are you?" I asked, my voice shaking.

"You can call me Megareus," he replied. "And you?"

"Aristion."

The man gave me a warm smile.

"I know you are feeling confused. All will become clear in time. However, we have a long journey ahead of us. Collect what you need from your hut, but don't take too long."

I shook my head.

"Thank you for helping, but I'd rather stay here." I replied. There was no way I was about to abandon my life and follow this stranger.

The man let out a sigh.

"Regrettably, I can't let you do that. You're probably already feeling the stirrings of hunger and soon those feelings will consume you. You'll become a danger to everyone you care about. You must come with me. I can teach you control."

The moment he said the word "hunger," I felt it. During my attempt to process the turn of events, I had been distracted from something lying just beneath the surface. It was as if his words had unleashed something in me that came on with an intensity that took me by surprise. My entire body was shaking with an uncontrollable desire to be satiated— something I could not define. What was happening to me?

Megareus must have noticed the look that had come over my face. He drew close and rested a hand on my shoulder.

"We cannot wait, you need to feed. The change has left you depleted." With that, he held out a wrist and placed it against my mouth.

"It's OK, take what you need," he said calmly.

It was as if the ability to reason had left me. One moment I was staring at the bulging veins in his forearm and the next I had locked onto it with my teeth. They penetrated and I began to drink.

~

Having just come from Sparta, where I had received a mixed reception, I was feeling a mixture of anger and frustration. They had been in the middle of a religious celebration, the *Festival of Carneia*. For the Spartan's, it was a sacrosanct period of peace and they were unwilling to interrupt their festivities to address the issue of the imminent Persian invasion. Eventually they had agreed to mobilize their army, but only after the full moon. That was over ten days away and would probably be too late.

The city-state of Sparta currently lacked any form of unified leadership. King Cleomenes had recently been forced into exile and then imprisoned after he had overthrown his co-king, Demaratus, for allegedly collaborating with the Persians. Sparta was still reeling from its internal battle for power and dominance.

How could they be so shortsighted? The only way to guarantee success against the invasion force would involve a combined response from both Sparta and Athens. It was not the time for heal dragging and petty squabbling.

With no immediate help forthcoming, I left and rode posthaste to meet with Miltiades, the Athenian general.

~

"Come in," the voice boomed.

I had been waiting for almost half a candle mark and experienced a surge of relief as I got to my feet and walked into the general's quarters.

Miltiades was leaning over his desk, both hands outstretched and resting on its finely engraved wood. He was poring over a large map. Standing patiently, I waited with my hands crossed in front of me. Eventually, the general looked up and a broad smile crossed his lips.

I had known him for around seven years. At the time, I had been acting as a mercenary and assisted him during the Ionian revolt against Persian rule. Doomed from the start, the revolt had eventually collapsed, leaving Miltiades with no choice but to flee with his family to Athens.

Miltiades had no knowledge of my true motivation. As was the nature of all vrykolakas, I was a master of subterfuge and could wear many masks. He knew that I was an excellent fighter—one of the best, but no more. To avoid drawing attention to myself, I exercised restraint when in the presence of others. I never displayed the full extent of my abilities. The only exception to this rule was in the case of someone I was about to kill.

"It's great to see you old friend," he said, beckoning me to sit.

"I wish it was under better circumstances," I replied, taking the empty chair. "I have some dire news from the east!"

The general grimaced and motioned for me to continue.

"There's a large Persian invasion fleet amassing. It was almost ready to set sail when I left. That was four days ago."

"Number?"

"600 hundred ships and an army of approximately 20,000—a mixture of cavalry and foot soldiers," I replied.

"Damn!"

"I've already contacted the Spartan's, but they were in the middle of one of their never-ending festivals and won't send help for at least ten days!"

The general groaned and looked down at the map. "Where did you see the fleet?"

I leaned over the table and pointed at a location on his map. It was a large bay on the eastern shore of what the Greeks called the *Mesogeios*.

Straightening, the general walked to the door, opened it and shouted for his assistant. "LYCUS!"

In the distance I heard a muffled reply, followed by footsteps that grew louder as the man approached.

"Yes sir?"

"Call for my commanders."

"Yes sir!"

"And send a messenger to Plataea telling them to mobilize their forces."

Returning into the room, Miltiades glanced at me. The expression on his bearded face was grim.

"Well, my friend, we have our work cut out for us. I'm assuming that you are willing to stay and help?"

"Of course, whatever you need," I replied without hesitation.

Miltiades slumped into the chair behind his desk and I began to elaborate on what I had discovered during my reconnaissance.

The meeting with Miltiades and his command team went on for hours. After much debate, it had drawn to a close and everyone had rushed into action. The atmosphere in the camp shifted from tense anticipation to frenetic energy. I could hear shouts in the distance as the camp mobilized and the men were called to arms. The clanging of weapons being distributed, the rhythmic thud of feet, and the rallying cries of officers echoed through the air. The scent of campfires mingled with the earthy smell of the terrain, creating a heady mix that heightened the sense of urgency and impending conflict.

Chapter Four

Aristion

490 BCE

I stood on a large hill overlooking the small town of Marathon, located in a large bay a few leagues from Athens. The terrain surrounding the town was rough, mountainous and swampland dominated much of the low-lying area. Over the past few years, the wetlands and its quicksand had proven to be treacherous, claiming many lives. Unwary travelers, those leaving the safety of the roads, had been sucked beneath its surface, never to be seen again.

The Persian fleet was anchored in the bay and their army had set up camp, completely engulfing the town. It was a stalemate. There were only two ways out of the bay and both had been blocked by large contingencies of the Athenian army.

Five days had now passed and Miltiades was growing impatient. He was hoping that enemy would provide him with an opening, one that would enable him to bring the conflict to a swift and decisive end. But none had been forthcoming.

"Look there!" he exclaimed, pointing at the large area of flat land just northeast of the town.

I focused my attention in the direction he was pointing. I could see more clearly and a great deal further than him. It was one of the many benefits afforded to me after I was born into my new life.

There was activity. The Persian cavalry was disbanding their camp and I could make out men leading their horses toward the beach. Shifting my vision out to sea, I saw a multitude of small boats heading toward shore.

"They are breaking camp!" I exclaimed.

Mitiades grunted in the affirmative and then a wicked smile crossed his face.

"They think to escape us—we shall see about that!"

He called to his messengers and was about to give them orders when I interrupted him. "Hold on—I think we should wait."

He turned back to me with a quizzical expression. "Why?"

"Once the majority of the cavalry has boarded, we could descend on their flanks from both sides and then crush their center. Without cavalry, they won't be able to stop us."

Mitiades paused to consider my suggestion and then slapped me on the back, laughing.

"This is why I like you!" he smiled.

Taking my suggestion, he relayed orders to the three messengers who had been waiting patiently. There was an air of excitement emanating from him. He lived to fight and it was in times like these that he truly shone.

"Want to see some action?"

"I thought you'd never ask," I replied with a grin.

"Go join the right flank. Try not to have too much fun!" he laughed.

~

A flaming signal arrow arched into the sky directly above the hill where Miltiades was located, its fiery tail a beacon of impending action. The air was thick with anticipation and the distant sounds of the Persian camp.

With a roar that seemed to shake the very ground, 10,000 Athenian soldiers descended from the hills like a tidal wave of bronze and crimson. Their armor glinted in the sunlight, and their battle cries filled the air, a fierce and determined chorus. The flanks of the Persian army, taken completely off guard, collapsed immediately under the onslaught. Shields clashed and swords struck, the chaotic symphony of battle echoing across the plain. Dust rose from the ground, mingling with the acrid smell of sweat and blood.

The Athenians then pressed toward the main body of the enemy, located on the edge of the town. The Persians, without the support of their cavalry, quickly fell into disarray. Panic spread like wildfire through their ranks as they struggled to maintain formation against the relentless Athenian assault. The sun beat down mercilessly, reflecting off the Athenian spears and helmets, creating a dazzling, intimidating display.

It was not long before the Persian lines broke completely, and the battle turned into a rout. The enemy, many dropping their weapons in terror, ran for their ships anchored offshore. Thousands were cut down, their cries of despair and the clash of metal a stark contrast to the earlier confidence of the Persian forces. The Athenians, fueled by the momentum of their initial success and the desire to defend their homeland, gave no quarter. They continued to advance with relentless determination, driving the remains of the shattered Persian force into the sea.

~

The sun had just dropped below the horizon as I picked my way through the sea of bodies, making my way to the Athenian command tent.

Mitiades was sitting at a table loaded with fresh meats, vegetables and fruit. In his hand was a mug of ale.

"Thanks for the invitation," I said, as I walked in.

"Sit… sit," he replied, motioning me to take a chair.

"Thank you, I'm starving!" I lied.

Although I enjoyed eating, it did not sustain me like blood. However, in that respect, I was already satiated. I had found a dying Persian soldier in an abandoned building on the edge of town, and the opportunity had been too good to pass up. After days of not feeding, it had come as a welcome relief. I now felt vital, alive, and energized, my strength renewed.

"I was hoping for a better fight!" Mitiades declared, as a piece of meat intended for his stomach fell from his mouth onto the table in front of him.

"We should count our blessings," I replied, as I watched him inhale his food. "If they had not attempted to leave, we would still be standing on that damn hill staring at their camp!"

"True, true!"

He took another mouthful of meat and washed it down with a swig of ale, not even bothering to chew.

Rather than letting him eat alone I picked up a turkey leg and began to gnaw at it.

"The last report put the enemy dead at over 6000," he said, taking another gulp of ale and placing the mug on the table.

"And ours?"

"Under 200," he replied gleefully.

I sat back and took a deep breath. The whole situation could have unfolded very differently. Of all the outcomes, we could not have wished for a better result.

We were then interrupted as a soldier entered the command tent.

"Sir, my apologies for the intrusion. We have just received a message from the Spartans. They will be arriving tomorrow afternoon."

We both stared at him blankly and then, turning our heads in unison, our eyes met and we roared with laughter.

Chapter Five

Kallian

482 BCE

Kallian awoke with a start. He had been dreaming and it took him a few seconds to adjust to his surroundings. His manhood was rock hard and he smiled as he recalled the erotic nature of the dream, his memory of it gradually fading as he regained consciousness.

He heard someone cough into their hand. Eioneus was standing in the doorway with a broad grin on his face, his naked bronze torso silhouetted by the bright light that was streaming in from behind.

"Hey little brother, it's time to wake up!"

Kallian groaned and closed his eyes.

"Why? We have a day off. All I want to do is sleep!"

"Sleep? It's a beautiful morning! I'm off to the river. Come join me!" he replied, glancing down Kallian's aroused shaft as he laid sprawled on the bed in front of him. "From what I can see it looks like you need to cool off anyway!" he added with a laugh.

"Fine!" Kallian groaned, sitting up and then getting to his feet.

Kallian was twenty years old. Thirteen years had passed since he had entered the *agōgē*, and the years of training had transformed him. He was no longer a boy. Now fully grown, his athletic physique was defined by lean, sinewy muscle, and he moved with the grace and agility of a predatory cat.

Grabbing his scabbard and sword, Kallian joined Eioneus at the door and the two men began the short hike to the river.

"It won't be long before I'm assigned to my new command," Eioneus remarked as they walked.

"I know. I hope they place me to the same unit," Kallian replied. "I'm going to miss you!"

Over the years, the two boys had grown close. Eioneus had been partnered with Kallian to assist with his training, and they had hit it off almost immediately. Not only did they have a lot in common, such as the loss of their parents at an early age, but they were also quick learners and had rapidly become masters of the sword, spear, and bow. Of all the boys at the *agōgē*, they were considered the best. None could match them.

"I'll put a word in with the officer in charge," Eioneus remarked.

"That would be great!" Kallian replied, beaming.

The river came into sight, its clear, glistening waters weaving a path through the lush landscape. The sunlight danced on the surface, creating a shimmering mosaic of light. The sound of the gently flowing water grew louder, mingling with the rustling leaves and the distant calls of birds.

Kallian and Eioneus glanced at each other and smiled, a shared look of excitement and camaraderie passing between them. The anticipation of the cool, refreshing embrace of the river was palpable.

"Race you!" Eioneus shouted, his voice filled with playful challenge.

Breaking into a sprint, Eioneus soon began to pull ahead. Kallian, with no desire to be left in the dust, jumped over the trunk of a fallen tree, detoured from the trail and took off down a steep slope. He slid most of the way, controlling his decent with one hand. Reaching the bottom, he quickly regained his footing, just as Eioneus rounded the bend to his right.

Kallian, now in the lead, leapt into motion and made short work of the remaining distance. He reached the river and without so much as a glance back, cast his sword aside and dove in headfirst.

Surfacing, Kallian glanced around. Eioneus was nowhere to be seen. It was then that he felt his legs being pulled from under him. With barely a moment to catch his breath, he was dragged under.

After few seconds, the two men were both laughing and coughing up water.

"You cheated!" Eioneus exclaimed, his face displaying a picture of mock indignation.

"No, you're just a sore loser," Kallian laughed, sweeping the wet hair from his face, so that it fell down his back.

"I still almost had you, even after your shortcut!"

As he spoke, Eioneus drew close to him. There was a wicked glint in his eye. Then, as quick as a mountain lion, he pounced, wrapping his arm around Kallian's neck. Within seconds the two men were thrashing around in the water, locked in combat.

After a few minutes, the struggle for dominance subsided, with neither gaining the upper hand. Both were laughing.

Eioneus grabbed Kallian, pulling him against his muscular torso. Their lips touched and within seconds they were locked in a soul-deep press of open mouths and tangled tongues.

~

Kallian watched as his friend emerged from the river, water streaming from his hair and down his bronze back. Taking in the magnificence of his body, his attention lingered on his firm muscular glutes, glistening in the sunlight, as he walked across the sand.

Eioneus came to a standstill and turned to face the sun. He stretched, arching back with his arms overhead, his long hard shaft curving out from his body as he did so.

Kallian felt an intense feeling of desire come over him. As he left the water to join Eioneus, he felt a stirring in his loins as his own manhood hardened—in anticipation of what was to come. Eioneus smiled as Kallian drew close.

They kissed and their bodies intertwined in an embrace. Kallian's hand drifted down Eioneus' lean, well-defined abs to the mass of black hair at his groin. He then took hold of the thick long muscle that was pressed up against him and pulsating with pleasure. Eioneus groaned and they both fell to the sand, still wrapped in each other's arms.

Kallian lost track of the time as they made love under the warm sun of the *Mesogeios.* He was in heaven.

With their mouths pressed together, Eioneus moaned as Kallian caressed the length of his shaft with his hand. The kissing became more frantic, more passionate. Finally, with one final cry of pleasure, Eioneus arched back and the life force exploded from him. The orgasm was so intense that his body continued to convulse for many beats of his racing heart, before subsiding into stillness.

Eioneus, then leaned into Kallian, their lips still touching. Although the tips of his fingers could not touch, they partially encircled Kallian's throbbing manhood. With one hand wrapped around its base, he began to rhythmically move the other along its length. As Kallian groaned, his breathing quickened and Eioneus' hand moved faster. It did not take long before the large muscle between Kallian's legs erupted, drenching his torso with beads of white.

Closing their eyes, the men collapsed back onto the sand, exhausted.

It could not have been more than a few seconds before the sound of a person clapping interrupted the silence.

"Finally, I thought you'd be at it forever!" a male voice boomed, the clapping fading as he spoke.

Startled, Kallian rolled onto his side, glanced up and locate the source of the disturbance. A man was sitting on the bank just above them.

"Agamedes! How long have you been there?" Kallian muttered through gritted teeth.

"Oh—a few minutes. I was enjoying the show!" he exclaimed, chuckling as he did so.

"You are insufferable. What do you want?"

"Grab your swords, you are both requested to attend the commander at the arena," he replied.

Kallian and Eioneus groaned in unison. So much for their day of relaxation.

Chapter Six

Aristion

482 BCE

Since I was fluent in both Greek and Farsi my master, Megareus, had assigned me to Greece. That had been 9 years ago. My mission was to assist the Greeks in their campaign to stave off the Persian expansion and address the threat posed to our kind by the Zoroastrian Warrior Clerics and their *mágos.*

My service to my master began the night of my turning. Seven decades had now passed, the first of which had been grueling. It had taken me time to adjust to my new life and a number of years to learn the art of control. There was no way a vrykolakas could blend into the world of humans without the ability to restrain its thirst for blood. A vrykolakas who did not have the ability of restraint, would pose a threat to our entire society—one that was cloaked in secrecy and existed in the shadows. If our existence became common knowledge, moving from the realm of folklore into one of fact, the human population would rise up and exterminate us. Our numbers were few and as strong as we were individually, we did not have the ability to withstand the tide of humankind if it united against us.

We had already drawn the attention of the Persians when, a few years earlier, a vrykolakas had rampaged through a remote Persian farming community and killed over 40 of its inhabitants.

Darius the Great, the third King of Kings of the Achaemenid dynasty of Persia, had responded by creating a sect within his military hierarchy, the Zoroastrian Warrior Clerics. Their sole mission was to hunt down and eradicate all vrykolakas from the face of the planet.

In order to protect our very existence, the vrykolakas council had come to a simple, but inevitable conclusion. The Achaemenid dynasty could not be allowed to expand its sphere of influence. To this end, it was decided that any assistance we could offer the Greeks would benefit both parties. They were the only military power with enough strength to halt the prolific expansion of the Persian Empire.

~

I had just met with King Leonidas I of Sparta. The constant threat of invasion was a source of great consternation and he'd requested my presence to discuss any measures that could be taken to protect the sovereignty of the land under his care.

Mounted on my white stallion, I arrived at the gates of the *agōgē*, just south of the Spartan capital.

"Halt! State your business," one of the two sentries demanded in a perfunctory tone.

"I am under the direct orders of King Leonidas and need to meet with your commander," I replied, pulling out a scroll from the pack slung over my shoulder and tossing it to him.

The man snatched it from the air, carefully broke its seal and read. Although his attitude had been initially cold, the contents of the scroll caused him to immediately change his demeanor.

"Yes sir! Proceed straight ahead and then turn right at the end of the promenade. His quarters will be directly in front of you," he stammered, coming to attention.

"Thank you."

I gave the reins a slight shake and my horse lurched into motion.

The promenade was wide and paved, lined with well-kept buildings made of sturdy white stone. The architecture was stark and functional, yet its simplicity exuded a certain majesty. Interspersed along its length were numerous statues of their gods—Zeus, Apollo, and Ares, to name but a few. These statues, though not overly elaborate, were meticulously crafted and conveyed a sense of power and reverence. I had been exposed to numerous cultures in my life, and the architecture of the Spartans, with its emphasis on practicality and strength, never ceased to amaze me. It was quite magnificent in its own austere way, reflecting the disciplined and resilient spirit of its people.

A few minutes later I was standing in front of the *agōgē's* commander, Thalysios. He was a muscular man, balding and looked to be in his late forties. On his lower body he wore *pteruges,* consisting of a double layer of stiffened, hardened leather flaps, which offered flexibility but also afforded protection in combat. His chest was covered by a finely engraved *linothorax,* a type of armor made of hardened leather. However, the most striking thing about his attire was the crimson cloak, an *ephaptis,* fastened to his shoulders by gold clasps. He was the epitome of a hardened Spartan veteran—the scars on his arms clearly confirming that he had seen a great deal of combat.

Handing the parchment back to me, he nodded thoughtfully and met my eyes.

"What exactly do you require?"

"I need one of your men. He must be able to think on his feet, fluent in Farsi and know how to handle a sword," I replied.

Thalysios nodded again and his forehead furrowed as he considered my request.

"I have a couple of good options. Join me for breakfast and then I'll introduce you," he replied. "In fact, I'll have them spar so that you can see them in action."

~

I was seated next to the commander on a hard wooden chair, its rough edges digging into my back. Below us was a circular arena lined with spectators, other trainees from the *agōgē,* their faces displaying eagerness for what was about to take place.

Two men walked out of an opening, situated between two buildings directly opposite us. Both were naked, save for the swords they carried, their bodies glistening with sweat. The tension in the air was palpable as they reached the center of the arena. There, they turned and tilted their heads in a gesture of readiness and respect to their commander. The crowd fell silent, the only sound being the faint rustle of the breeze and the distant murmur of voices.

"This will be a pleasure to watch. They are the elite of my recruits and well matched."

The commander raised his hand, paused and then dropped it in a signal for them to begin.

Immediately, the two combatants leapt into action. The shorter of the two, a lean, muscled young man, lunged forward, his blade weaving an intricate circular pattern that was both fast and precise.

The other stepped to the right, pivoting as he did so, causing his adversary's initial thrust to pass harmlessly by his left shoulder. He then struck back, but the shorter combatant quickly reversed his grip and brought his *xiphos* up in a diagonal upward motion. There was a loud ringing as their double-edged iron swords met.

The men quickened their pace, their movements fluid as they swung, blocked and parried, their swords ringing out as they made contact. It was a sight to behold. Both moved with a practiced agility and grace, engaged in an exquisite dance for domination.

After a few minutes, with neither gaining the upper hand, the men stepped back and began to circle each other.

"Is that the best you've got?" the youth chided the taller man, grinning as he did so.

The comment appeared to goad the other into action. He began to close the distance between them and then broke into a run.

Their swords met as the taller of the two brought his *xiphos* down in a slicing arc, only to be blocked by the youth's blade. He then pivoted and lashed out with his foot forcing the younger man to sidestep to avoid being hit.

Without a moment of hesitation, the younger of the two stepped inside the other's guard, spinning as he did so and grabbed his sword arm. In a twisting motion he brought the arm up over his shoulder, simultaneously turning his back and leaning over, taking the arm with him. The man was pulled off his feet, over the young fighters back and landed hard on the dirt. Before he had a chance to recover there was a blade was at his neck.

"Do you yield?"

"Yes!" the man groaned.

The other grabbed his hand, pulled him to his feet and both turned to the commander, raising their swords in a salute.

"What do you think?" Thalysios inquired, glancing over at me.

"Excellent, I like him!" I replied.

"Which one?"

"The younger one—the winner of the contest."

Thalysios motioned for the men to approach. They climbed the short flight of stone stairs to the marble pavilion and came to a halt directly in front of us. The pavilion, with its ornate columns and intricate carvings, provided a regal backdrop to the scene.

"What's your name?" I inquired, looking directly at him, my eyes meeting his with a steady gaze.

"Kallian, sir," he responded, standing tall and composed.

"Good job. I like the way you fight!" I said, my tone appreciative and firm.

"Thank you, sir," Kallian replied, a hint of pride in his voice.

I then switched to Farsi, my words fluid and deliberate. "Tell me a little of your capabilities."

Kallian straightened slightly, his expression confident. "I am a master of sword, spear, and bow. I am also skilled in the art of *pankration*," he replied in fluent Farsi, his voice carrying the assurance of experience.

I nodded in approval, impressed by his versatility. *Pankration* was a deadly form of martial art that combined boxing, wrestling, kicking, joint manipulation, choke holds, and submission techniques. It was a discipline that required not only physical strength but also strategic cunning and resilience.

"Anything else?"

Kallian glanced at Thalysios. He seemed reluctant to elaborate.

"He's hesitant to speak of it, but he's almost completed his training to join the *Krypteia*," Thalysios interrupted, also speaking Farsi.

I could not have wished for a better recruit. Only the elite of the *agōgē* were assigned to the *Krypteia.* The organization boasted an extensive network of spies and assassins. Its members also worked to maintain order, patrolling the Spartan countryside and frontier borders, gathering intelligence as they did so.

Looking at Kallian, I appraised him one last time. Having made my decision, I glanced at Thalysios.

"He's exactly what I require. I'll take him, if that's alright with you?"

"Of course!" Thalysios replied with a smile.

I turned back to the men standing before us. It was gone in an instant, but I was sure that I'd seen a momentary flash of distress in their eyes.

Before I had time to contemplate what I had just witnessed, Thalysios stood up and dismissed the two warriors.

"Since you will be here for the rest of the day, let me give you a tour of our fine *agōgē*!"

"That would be wonderful," I replied, glancing back at the two warriors as they exited the arena.

Chapter Seven

Kallian

482 BCE

A rooster crowed in the distance, heralding the dawn. Kallian gradually opened his eyes, his gaze settling on Eioneus, who was wrapped around him. The early morning light cast a soft glow through the window, illuminating Eioneus's serene face. Kallian gently swept the mop of black curly hair from his eyes and then kissed him gently on the lips.

"Good morning," Kallian whispered, his voice tender.

Eioneus responded with a gentle brush of his hand against Kallian's cheek, his touch lingering as if to memorize every detail.

"I can't believe you're leaving," he whispered, a hint of sadness lacing his voice, his eyes reflecting a mixture of sorrow and resignation.

"Me either," Kallian replied, his heart heavy with the weight of their imminent separation.

"I guess we knew this day would come," Eioneus continued, his voice barely above a whisper, each word carrying the burden of their shared past and uncertain future.

"I know, I just wish it wasn't so soon!" Kallian said, his voice breaking slightly as he spoke. The urgency of their situation pressed upon them both, making every moment feel painfully fleeting.

Eioneus leaned into Kallian and embraced him tightly, their bodies entwined as if they could merge into one and halt the passage of time. Neither wanted to let go, their shared warmth a comforting balm against the chill of impending absence. Time felt suspended, each heartbeat echoing the depth of their bond, but Kallian knew he had to prepare for his departure.

Reluctantly, they broke contact, the separation a physical pain that left them both feeling hollow. Both men slumped onto their backs, the coolness of the sheets a stark contrast to the warmth they had shared. They stared vacantly at the ceiling in silence, the unspoken words hanging heavily in the air. The quietude of the room was filled with the sound of their synchronized breathing, a temporary solace before the inevitable goodbye.

The room around them, filled with the familiar objects of their life together, seemed to blur at the edges, their focus solely on the weight of the moment. Eioneus's hand sought out Kallian's, their fingers intertwining in a final gesture of connection. As the first rays of the sun spilled over the horizon, they knew that this dawn was the beginning of a new and challenging chapter, one they had to face apart.

~

Kallian had been assigned a horse from the *agōgē* stables and left with Aristion just after breakfast. They were now heading north on their way to the Athenian port of Piraeus.

He was still reeling from the drastic turn of events over the past 24 hours. Less than a day ago, he had been making love with Eioneus on the sandy banks of the Eurotas, without a care in the world. Now, he was on a horse in the company of a stranger, leaving behind his life at the *agōgē*—the only life he had ever known. The sudden upheaval was disorienting, but it was the heaviness in his heart over the loss of Eioneus that weighed on him the most. The memories of their time together, the warmth of Eioneus's touch, and the bond they shared seemed like a distant dream now. The thought of never seeing Eioneus again filled him with an overwhelming sense of grief and longing, making the uncertainty of his new journey even harder to bear.

"Where are we going?" Kallian inquired.

"We are scheduled to depart on a ship sailing from Piraeus." Aristion replied.

"Can you tell me a little about our mission?"

Aristion did not answer immediately. He appeared to be lost in thought, his brow furrowed as he gazed into the distance. Eventually, he looked over at Kallian, his eyes serious.

"I guess this is as good a time as any. We are going to Sardis, the former capital of the Kingdom of Lydia."

Kallian was shocked. "That's in Persian territory," he exclaimed.

"I'm happy to see that you know your geography," Aristion replied, smiling wryly.

"Why—what?" the words stumbling out of him. Aristion laughed.

"We will be on an intelligence gathering mission. Just to warn you, we may be there for a number of years!"

Kallian was dumfounded. Never would he have imagined that his work, as a member of the *Krypteia*, would take him behind Persian lines.

"We need to discuss your role. It is integral to your disguise," Aristion continued. "It's essential that we blend in and don't draw attention."

"Yes, yes—I totally understand," Kallian stammered.

This was a lot for Kallian to take in and he was beginning to question if he was up to the task. As well trained as he was, a single mistake on his part could result in their death.

"I will be acting as a wealthy merchant, and you will be my assistant," Aristion continued. "Our first task will be to locate a small shop in the city to purchase. Once set up, your primary responsibility will be to manage the business while I am out gathering intelligence. It is essential that we operate just like any other business. That's why I need someone to assist me."

Kallian listened intently as Aristion spoke, his brow furrowed in concentration.

When we get to Athens, we'll take a day to gather supplies. Plus, you'll need new clothing, something appropriate for the role you'll be playing, not like the *pteruges* you are wearing!" he said with a grin, glancing down at the leather protection around Kallian's lower body.

This was the first time in his life that Kallian had worn the clothing of a Spartan warrior. During his many years of training, he'd been naked—his sole possession a *phoinikis,* a red cloak. He liked his new garb. It marked the completion of his schooling at the *agōgē*—a badge of honor, so to speak. Now, within a matter of hours, he would have to switch it out for something that was typical for a citizen of the Achaemenid dynasty of Persia. Well—shit!

"I guess I'll need a new name to go with my new clothing?"

Aristion appeared to think on it for a few seconds and then his face lit up.

"How about Farbod?" he remarked with a broad smile. "NO!"

Aristion laughed.

"It's not so bad, it means the protector of glory. Very befitting don't you think?"

"NO! I'm not going to live out the next few years called Farbod!"

Aristion was obviously teasing him, and Kallian couldn't help but smile. Despite the whirlwind of events and the uncertainty of the future, this light-hearted banter was a welcome relief. Aristion's humor and easy- going nature were beginning to break through Kallian's initial wariness. The gentle ribbing about his attire made him feel a sense of camaraderie he hadn't expected. Kallian was already beginning to like the man, finding comfort in the way Aristion balanced seriousness with levity.

"How familiar are you with the geography and customs of the Persian Empire?"

"I was given extensive lessons in their military structure, customs, and history," Kallian replied. "I am also familiar with the geography of both Greece and the lands held by the Achaemenid dynasty. I guess the term *'Know thy enemy'* was the motivating force behind much of my teaching."

Aristion chucked. "You are familiar with Sun Tzu?"

"Yes. We don't have a great deal of knowledge regarding the Zhou Dynasty of China, but my *agōgē* had a translation of *The Art of War*. It was required reading. I loved it and have read it countless times!" Kallian's eyes lit up with enthusiasm as he spoke about the ancient text. "The strategies and philosophies it contains have always fascinated me. I believe they can be applied to many aspects of life, not just warfare."

Aristion was impressed. There was much more to this warrior than exceptional fighting skills. Kallian's intellect and thirst for knowledge were evident, and his appreciation for such a profound work revealed a depth of character and insight that Aristion had not fully anticipated. He realized that Kallian's disciplined mind and strategic thinking would be invaluable assets in their mission. This young man was not just a product of rigorous training but also a thinker, a strategist, and a scholar in his own right. Aristion felt a growing sense of respect and admiration for his new companion.

They then rode in silence for a while, the rhythmic sound of their horses' hooves blending with the rustling leaves and distant bird calls. Sunlight filtered through the canopy above, casting dappled patterns on the forest floor. The scent of pine and wildflowers filled the air, creating a serene atmosphere as they continued down the trail. Eventually, Aristion spoke again.

"Back to your name. How about Pabag?"

Kallian groaned, a mix of exasperation and amusement. "NO!" he replied emphatically, grinning.

Chapter Eight

Aristion

482 BCE

I stepped back and looked Kallian up and down with a speculative eye. He was wearing *shalvar's*—full-length Persian style pants and a cream-colored kaftan, tunic, that reached just past his knees. Around his waist was a wide leather belt.

Kallian let out a curse. He was struggling with a long piece of cloth made of cotton that he was attempting, without much success, to bind around his head. After a few attempts, he turned to me, apparently satisfied.

"Is this correct?" he questioned.

I took one look at him and burst into laughter.

"The whole purpose of our attire is to blend in. One look at that disaster on your head and they'll imprison you for making a mockery of their national costume!" I replied, still chuckling.

Just as I spoke, the entire headdress unraveled and fell to the ground. "

Damn!" Kallian shouted, following it up with a series of colorful expletives, some of which were completely unfamiliar to me.

"Let me show you."

I walked over to him, picked up the piece of cloth, and began to carefully wrap it around his head. "This is called a *sarband*," I explained as I worked, my fingers deftly looping the fabric. "It's a type of headband or turban, traditionally worn to keep sweat out of your eyes and to shield you from the harsh sun."

As I adjusted the folds, ensuring they lay smoothly, I continued, "The *sarband* also carries symbolic significance. It can denote one's status, tribe, or even profession in some cultures. It's more than just a practical accessory."

I made sure the cloth was snug but not too tight, arranging it to cover his forehead and the back of his neck, where the sun's rays could be most unforgiving. "There, that should do it," I said, stepping back with a satisfied nod, admiring the way the *sarband* now framed his face, offering both protection and a touch of elegance.

"Well—I don't know how they fight wearing so much clothing? I feel like an Egyptian mummy swaddled in cloth. Why don't you just tie my hands behind my back while you're at it!"

I grinned.

"Oh, I assure you, they make it work. The Persians are excellent fighters!"

"I guess I'll see for myself soon enough. I'm just not used to wearing clothing, let alone so much of it—especially in combat," Kallian replied.

Done with his head attire, I turned Kallian towards a mirror made of polished bronze and stepped back.

"What do you think?"

"Ugh—I guess I look the part," Kallian replied with a grimace.

I paid the storekeeper and we left the little shop. There was a mass of humanity around us, swarming like bees around a honey pot, as we walked up a long flight of steps and past a statue of Athena.

"We have one more stop."

"What for?" Kallian inquired, his eyes roaming, taking in the bustling sights of the city. The streets were alive with activity, vendors shouting their wares, children darting through the crowds, and the scent of exotic spices filling the air.

"A bladesmith. You won't be able to take your *xiphos* with you. We need to purchase something more appropriate for your new role."

Kallian nodded in agreement, his eyes lighting up with enthusiasm. He even broke into a grin, the corners of his mouth lifting as a sense of excitement washed over him. Unlike clothing, which he had little interest in, swords were a different matter entirely. His passion for weaponry was evident in the way he carried himself, and the prospect of visiting a bladesmith ignited a spark of joy within him.

"It's not far. Just down that street to the right," I said, pointing toward a narrow alley lined with merchant stalls.

A few minutes later, we arrived at the entrance of one of the finest bladesmiths in Athens. The shop was modest from the outside, with a simple wooden sign bearing the image of a crossed sword and hammer. The rhythmic sound of metal striking metal echoed from within, a testament to the craftsmanship happening inside.

As we stepped through the door, the familiar scent of burning coal and hot iron filled the air. The interior was dimly lit, with walls adorned with an impressive array of swords, daggers, and other finely crafted weapons. Each blade reflected the flickering light from the forge, showcasing the meticulous detail and skill of their maker.

The bladesmith, a burly man with arms like tree trunks and a face weathered by years of intense labor, looked up from his anvil. His eyes, sharp and discerning, recognized me immediately. This was the man who had forged the *shamshir* that now hung at my waist—a weapon of exceptional quality that had served me well through countless battles and skirmishes.

"Aristion!" the man bellowed, with a broad smile.

"It's been a long time old friend!" I replied.

"At least eight years if I'm correct—and you don't look a day older— the Goddess Aphrodite must be shining on you!"

I grimaced inside, but the smile never left my face. It would only be a matter of time before I'd have to leave Greece for good. People would begin to question the eternal nature of my youthful looks.

"Kallian, this is Alkamenos," I announced, clapping the swordsmith on the back in a friendly gesture.

Alkamenos, a jovial man with a thick beard and a wide smile, reached out and took Kallian's hand in a firm grip, shaking it enthusiastically. The warmth of his welcome was as robust as his physique, forged by years at the anvil.

"It's a pleasure to meet you!" he exclaimed, his voice booming with genuine friendliness. "Come, come—take a seat. Can I offer you gentlemen a drink?"

Without waiting for an answer, he pulled out a flagon from under the counter along with three mugs, each bearing intricate designs of mythical creatures. He filled each mug to the brim with a rich, amber liquid that smelled of honey and spices.

"Here's to good friends and fine iron," Alkamenos declared, raising his mug in a toast. The sincerity in his eyes mirrored the craftsmanship of the weapons that surrounded us. With a hearty laugh, he knocked back the entire contents of his mug in three gulps, the sound of his enjoyment echoing in the small shop.

Kallian and I followed suit, raising our mugs and savoring the drink, which was as smooth and potent as the swordsmith's reputation.

As we set our empty mugs down, Alkamenos leaned back, his eyes twinkling with curiosity. "So, what brings you to my humble abode today?" he asked, already knowing it was more than just a social call.

"Kallian needs a sword." I replied.

"Ah—what do you have in mind?"

"We would like to switch out his *xiphos* for something like a Persian *akīnaka*. Do you have anything like that in your collection?"

An *akīnaka* was a Persian double-edged short sword made of bronze or iron. I wanted Kallian to have a weapon that was similar in style to his *xiphos*, something he was familiar with. I did not have time for him to master a completely different weapon.

Alkamenos scratched his beard thoughtfully and then nodded. "Yes, I have just the thing," he said, his eyes lighting up with excitement, before walking to the back of the shop and opening a cupboard.

Moments later, he returned with a cloth bundle and placed it on the table in front of us. He then carefully unwrapped it to reveal a beautifully crafted weapon. The blade was expertly forged, its double edges gleaming with lethal sharpness. The hilt was intricately designed, fitting comfortably in the hand, and the balance was impeccable.

"This," Alkamenos said, the pride evident in his voice, "is one of my finest works. It's based on the Persian *akīnaka* but with some enhancements in durability and grip. It should feel familiar in your hand, Kallian, much like your *xiphos*."

Kallian's expression radiated approval as he inspected the weapon before him.

"Pick it up—get a feel for it," Alkamenos suggested, making eye contact with Kallian and gesturing toward the sword.

Kallian nodded in reply and picked up the weapon, testing its weight and balance, before walking into an open space. Coming to a standstill, he took a deep breath and then began an elegant set of well-practiced movements the Greeks called a *pyrriche*. He was light on his feet, and the swings of the sword were precise and graceful. The moves became quicker and quicker, and the sword blurred as he lunged, parried, and pivoted.

We watched in silence, entranced by the display. Kallian's fluid movements were a testament to his skill and training, each step and swing blending seamlessly into the next. His eyes focused intensely on an invisible opponent, reflecting his concentration and mastery of the art. The air around him seemed to hum with the energy of his performance, the blade slicing through it with a sharp, clean sound.

Kallian's pace then began to gradually slow before he finally came to a halt, bringing the weapon to a guard position. His breathing was steady, and his stance unwavering, showcasing the weapon's flawless integration into his combat style.

"That was beautiful to watch," Alkamenos remarked with a smile. "I can't think of a better owner for this fine weapon!"

"Thank you," Kallian replied, beaming. "The sword is flawless and perfectly balanced!"

The more Aristion got to know the lad, the more he liked him. He had definitely made the right choice. Lithe, skilled and sharp of wits, Kallian was perfect for the mission that awaited them.

"How much?" I inquired, glancing at the swordsmith.

Alkamenos scratched the side of his head, taking a few seconds of deliberation before replying. "I'll take his *xiphos* and five drachma."

I was surprised by his response. The weapon was worth at least double. "Thank you—that's really generous!"

"I'm just happy that the sword has found a good home," Alkamenos responded, grinning from ear to ear. "How about another drink before you depart?"

"Of course, it will give us time to catch up!" I replied, rummaging through my coin purse. I pulled out five drachma and handed them to him with a smile.

Alkamenos accepted the coins with a nod of appreciation. "Let's celebrate, then!" he exclaimed, reaching under the counter to retrieve the flagon and mugs once more.

~

With a final wave to Alkamenos, we left his shop and began to weave our way back through the bustling streets to the inn where we were staying. The city was alive with activity, vendors calling out their wares, and the aroma of street food mingling with the scent of the sea.

As we entered the crowded common room of the inn, we were greeted by a warm, lively atmosphere. The room was spacious, with low wooden beams and walls adorned with tapestries depicting various heroic tales. A large hearth crackled at one end, the flames casting a welcoming glow and a comfortable warmth.

Rough-hewn tables and benches filled the space, each occupied by travelers and locals alike, sharing food, drink, and stories. The air was thick with the mingled scents of roasted meat, fresh bread, and spiced wine. A minstrel played a lively tune on a lute in the corner, his music almost drowned out by the hum of conversation and occasional bursts of laughter.

I spied the innkeeper, a stout man with a friendly demeanor, and walked over to him. His eyes twinkled as he recognized us, wiping his hands on his apron before extending one in greeting.

"We would like to clean up before we dine. Where is the nearest bathhouse?"

"You're in luck—we have one attached to the inn. Just take the corridor on the far side of the room, exit the door at the end and the baths will be directly in front of you."

"Perfect! We will dine in about an hour. What's on the menu?"

"My wife has made a venison stew with root vegetables. There is also a selection of cold meats and sweetbreads," he replied, before turning to another patron who was waiting patiently for another drink.

A few minutes later Kallian and I were stripping off our clothing. I could not wait to wash away the dirt and grime from our day on the road. We then plunged into a pool of cool water.

Standing neck deep, I glanced around the room, taking in its architecture. As with most buildings of Athens, the structure was beautiful. The floor was made of polished marble and the room was lined with stone pillars and a number of stone benches. In the center there were two rectangular soaking areas, one hot and one cold.

Kallian switched to the hot pool and completely immersed himself, his head disappearing under the water.

Surfacing, he shook his head and swept his long black hair away from his face.

"This is quite a change from the Eurotas," he exclaimed. "I've never been to a bathhouse or bathed in hot water. We had to use the river, even in the middle of winter!"

I chuckled.

"It's probably the last chance we'll get to soak before we get to Sardis, so take your time," I replied, amusement evident in my voice.

Kallian responded with a broad grin and then slowly sank back beneath the surface.

Chapter Nine

Kallian

482 BCE

Kallian and Aristion were strategically positioned on a large outcropping of rock overlooking the sprawling city of Sardis. From their vantage point, the city unfolded beneath them, its winding streets and bustling markets alive with activity.

They had been traveling for five days—two aboard a small merchant ship, where the salty sea air and rhythmic rocking had become a constant companion, and three on horseback, traversing rugged terrain.

Kallian dismounted and stretched, feeling the tightness in his muscles. It had been the longest time he had ever spent in a saddle. Most of his rigorous training at the *agōgē* had been on foot, and he was not accustomed to the constant jostling and pressure of horseback riding. His legs felt stiff, and his back ached from the unfamiliar strain. He rolled his shoulders and took a deep breath, appreciating the solidity of the ground beneath his feet.

"Damn all these clothes to hell," he muttered, wiping the sweat from his eyes. "I feel like I'm trussed up like a boar at harvest festival and being baked alive!"

You'll get used to it!" Aristion laughed.

Sardis looked magnificent. Strategically located on a spur at the foot of Mount Tmolus, it commanded the central plain of the Hermus Valley and the western terminus of the Persian Royal Road.

The Royal Road had been built by Darius I of the Achaemenid Empire to facilitate rapid communication throughout his domain—from Susa to Sardis. Mounted couriers of the *Angarium*, the imperial postal system established by the Achaemenid Empire, could travel the 1800-mile journey in nine days, as opposed to the ninety it would take on foot. The service utilized relay stations and fresh horses at intervals along the route, allowing messengers to maintain high speeds and ensure swift delivery of messages across the vast empire.

Sardis had begun its life as a hilltop citadel—the home of the king of Lydia. Overtime, it had grown in size into a two-part town: the lower, located along the banks of the Pactolus, housing the ordinary citizens, and the upper, for the wealthy, along with the palace and royal households.

Fifteen years prior to their arrival, there had been a massive revolt against Persian control. The Ionians, with support from Athenian and Eretrian troops, had marched on Sardis, capturing and burning the city to the ground. This bold act of defiance was only the beginning of a prolonged and bloody conflict. For six arduous years, battles raged across the region, with heavy casualties on both sides. Ultimately, the Persian army, with its superior numbers and resources, prevailed and crushed the rebellion.

Over the years since the revolt, much of Sardis had been meticulously rebuilt. From what they could see, there was little evidence of the devastation that had once ravaged the city.

"Let's go, I want to get there before dark," Aristion said, as he turned and walked back to the horses that were grazing in an area of tall grass. His voice held a sense of urgency, driven by the fading daylight and the need to reach their destination safely.

Kallian took one last look at the city, its skyline tinged with the warm hues of the setting sun. He sighed, reluctant to mount his horse again. Every part of him ached from the grueling three-day ride, the hard saddle having left him sore and weary. Nonetheless, he followed Aristion, knowing they had little choice but to press on.

As they made their way down the dirt trail that led to the wide-open plain that surrounded the city, Kallian's curiosity got the better of him.

"When we were at sea you mentioned that you'd been here before."

"Yes, I was with Miltiades and the Athenian contingent during the uprising that sacked Sardis."

"It's a shame that the revolt failed," Kallian remarked.

"I know, but in hindsight, there had been little chance of success. The city would have been hard to hold, given its close proximity to the bulk of the Persian Empire," Aristion replied.

Kallian paused, considering how to continue with his line of questioning. "You must have been really young—the Ionian revolt took place a decade ago?"

"Yes—it was the first major campaign of my life," Aristion replied, lying.

The fact was, Aristion had been involved in battles against the expansion of the Achaemenid Empire for almost three decades. His first mission had been during the early part of Darius' reign and the Persian Empire's campaign against the Scythians. Kallian had not even been alive at the time.

Aristion felt his muscles tense at the youth's probing. This would probably be his last mission in which he directly assisted the Greeks before he had to disappear.

"How did you meet Miltiades?" Kallian asked, changing the subject.

"I joined his unit and helped him escape after the revolt collapsed," Aristion responded, deciding it was time to change the subject. "We're almost there. Do you have your cover story memorized?"

"Yes!"

Aristion nodded and gave Kallian an encouraging smile.

A few minutes later, they arrived at the main gate of the lower part of the city. The gate was imposing, made of thick, reinforced wood bound with iron, and flanked by high stone walls. Above, the city's crest was prominently displayed, a symbol of its Persian rulers. The gateway itself was bustling with activity, a steady stream of people entering and exiting under the watchful eyes of the guards.

Two guards, wearing the distinctive livery of the Persian army, stood at their posts, questioning everyone who passed through. Their uniforms were adorned with intricate patterns and symbols, and their helmets gleamed in the sunlight. Each guard held a spear in one hand and had a short sword sheathed at their side, ready for any trouble.

"Halt! State your business," one of the guards demanded, his voice firm and authoritative.

"We are here for *Paitishahem Gahambar,"* Aristion replied, speaking in fluent Farsi.

The guard nodded and waved them through. The festival attracted many followers of the Zoroastrian faith, who gathered for a five-day period of joyous celebration. The Persians believed that *Ahura Mazda*, the God of Zoroastrianism, had created the universe in six phases, each commemorated with a festival spanning several days. *Paitishahem Gahambar*, representing the creation of water, took the form of a grand harvest feast.

"First on the agenda—an inn!" Aristion proclaimed. "I need to eat and enjoy a few mugs of their best ale!"

"You won't get any objection from me!" Kallian replied with a grin.

Chapter Ten

Aristion

482 BCE

We were now standing in the foyer of the third inn we had visited, the other two having turned us away. Finding a room for the night had quickly become a bigger challenge than the grueling journey we had just completed, and our patience was wearing thin.

The inn's foyer was modestly decorated, with a worn but clean wooden counter and a few simple chairs for waiting guests. A flickering oil lamp cast a warm glow, creating a welcoming yet humble atmosphere.

"Do you have a vacancy? Two rooms would be preferable?" I inquired with a smile, trying to mask my frustration.

"I'm sorry sir, the inn is full."

"Ah—do you know where we may find lodging?"

The innkeeper, a portly man with a thick, graying beard, scratched his head and thought for a few seconds. His apron, stained with the evidence of countless meals prepared, hung loosely over his ample belly.

"Well, you could try the upper city. The accommodations up there are more expensive and are more likely to have vacancies. You won't have much luck down here. The city is bursting at its seams with people in town for *Paitishahem Gahambar*."

I nodded and expressed my thanks. The upper city was not my first choice, as I preferred to keep a low profile. However, we were now out of options and had little choice in the matter.

~

Unlike the wooden structures of the lower city, the inn in the upper city was an impressive stone edifice, almost palatial in comparison to the three that had turned us away. Its grand facade featured intricately carved pillars and a wide staircase leading to an imposing entrance. The windows were adorned with elegant shutters, and the roof was topped with gleaming tiles.

Inside, the opulence continued. The lobby was spacious, with marble floors that gleamed under the light of crystal chandeliers. Rich tapestries depicting scenes of myth and history adorned the walls, and the air was filled with the scent of fresh flowers arranged in large, ornate vases.

This inn held the status of the best in the city, and the nightly price definitely reflected its luxury. It was a stark contrast to the simpler inns of the lower city, but at this point, comfort would come as a welcome boon, given the hardship our journey.

"Take a couple of hours to settle in and bathe if you feel so inclined. I'll meet you in the dining hall in a couple of hours."

"OK—where are you going?" Kallian replied, with a quizzical expression on his face.

"Just a few errands. I'll be back soon."

The fact was, I needed to feed. I could last about ten days without consuming blood and eight had already passed. After that, fatigue would begin to debilitate me and my mental capacity would rapidly deteriorate, along with my ability to control my thirst. If that happened, disaster would ensue, not only for myself, but also for the residents of the surrounding neighborhood.

I made my way down the road to the lower city, wanting to put as much distance between myself and the inn as possible. Within a few minutes, I passed through a gate, and the stone structures gave way to a colorful array of buildings made of timber. They came in all shapes and sizes and were in varying states of repair. The streets were lined with market stalls, featuring colorful awnings to protect them from the occasional rain shower. Hundreds of festival goers were going about their business—some carrying baskets of goods they had purchased, while others haggled with the numerous merchants selling their wares.

The first order of operation would be to find a place to feed, somewhere private. I spied an ally off to my right and headed directly for it, almost running into an old woman whose attention was focused on a merchant selling clothing, rather than on the street in front of her.

The alley was narrow, with several branches splitting off in different directions. I chose one and, before long, found what I was looking for. The passage ended in a dead-end, directly in front of an abandoned building in a state of complete disrepair. From what I could tell, there was no sign of life. Satisfied, I retraced my steps back to the crowded street.

I stood patiently and watched the mass of humanity as it passed me by. I needed someone who was alone.

"Excuse me sir, could you give me directions to the closest inn?"

I turned to find a man who appeared to be in his late 20's. He was wearing a white *sarband*, *shalvar's* and a colorful robe. Slung across his back was a pack. He looked exhausted.

I could not believe my good fortune. Rather than having to seek out my next meal, my meal had found me!

"You're in luck. I was about to head back to my inn." I replied, giving the lad a warm smile.

Motioning for him to follow, we made our way down the alley. As we took the turning that led to the abandoned building, he slowed and came to a halt.

"Actually, it's OK, thanks for your help," he squeaked. "I need to grab some supplies at the market first."

I turned and looked at him.

"YOU HAVE NOTHING TO FEAR. FOLLOW ME!"

His eyes glazed over and all signs of resistance immediately vanished. He was now completely under my control. My master had spent years training me in the art of mesmerization and I excelled at it. It was one of the many gifts that came with being a vrykolakas.

With the dazed youth stumbling after me, I walked down the alley and into the abandoned building.

"LAY DOWN AND CLOSE YOUR EYES!"

He did so immediately.

I knelt next to the man as he lay unconscious, his pulse faint but steady. My senses heightened, I could hear the rush of blood in his veins, a tantalizing promise of strength. Two incisors, the telltale sign of all vrykolakas, extended from the top row of my teeth. They gleamed in the moonlight as I leaned closer.

With a swift, practiced motion, I bit into the large vein on the side of his neck. The skin gave way easily, and the warm, rich blood flowed into my mouth. Energy and vitality flooded into me as I drank, each gulp invigorating every fiber of my being. The man's life force was potent, and I could feel my strength returning, my senses sharpening with every pulse of his heart. His essence was like a revitalizing elixir, erasing the fatigue of the long journey and rejuvenating my weary body.

The taste was intoxicating, a mix of iron and life itself, and I felt a primal satisfaction in the act. My grip on his shoulders tightened momentarily as I took in the life-sustaining liquid, then slowly, I eased back, retracting my fangs and sealing the puncture wounds with a swipe of my tongue.

I stood up, feeling the power coursing through my veins, the world around me now more vivid and alive. The man would recover, albeit weakened, while I was renewed, ready to face whatever challenges lay ahead.

Glancing down at the prone you, I gave him a final command, "AFTER TWENTY BREATHS YOU WILL OPEN YOUR EYES AND GO ABOUT YOUR DAY. YOU WILL REMEMBER NOTHING OF WHAT HAS TRANSPIRED!"

~

Mission accomplished, I made my way back to the inn. Since I was done much sooner than expected, I was looking forward to a long soak before dinner.

I walked into the large bathing hall, located in a building adjacent to the inn where we were staying. Kallian was lying on the stone walkway that surrounded a pool of steaming water. His eyes were shut and his lips partially open, with a hint of a smile. There was an indescribable glow on his face. I stood in silence and took the opportunity to explore every aspect of his lean athletic body, taut with sinewy muscle from his years of training at the *agōgē*. He was beautiful.

Although I had been aware of my attraction to men since my early teens, my first encounter with someone of the same sex had not taken place until 30 years after my turning. The affair had been brief, since my lover had died a few months after we met. A plague had decimated the community in which he lived and he'd been one of first to fall victim. Regrettably, I'd been away at the time, or I would have attempted to save his life by turning him.

His death had hit me hard, leaving a void that seemed impossible to fill. Since then, I had been hesitant to open myself up to any form of intimate contact, especially with a mortal. Their lives burned bright but brief, like candles flickering in the wind, while I was condemned to an existence that stretched on interminably. The thought of forming another bond, only to watch it wither and fade, was more than I could bear. It was easier, safer, to keep my distance and shroud myself in the solitude that had become my refuge.

Yet, in the quiet moments, I couldn't help but yearn for the warmth of companionship, the solace of a shared touch. The dichotomy of my existence—desiring closeness but fearing loss—was a constant, gnawing presence in my mind. It was a cruel irony, to live forever and yet be perpetually haunted by the transient nature of those I might come to care for.

As I took in the beauty of my companion, my eyes settled on the muscle between his legs. It was large and perfectly proportioned, just like the rest of his athletic physique. Transfixed, I began to feel a stirring in my loins. It had been a long time since I'd felt an intense desire for anything except blood. However, the feeling also brought about a conflict within me. This was not something I could give myself over to. I knew, all too well, where this path would take me.

Averting my gaze, I stripped off my clothing and jumped into the pool of warm water.

"You're back!" Kallian exclaimed, as I surfaced. "Did everything go well?"

"Yes, very well," I replied, giving him a broad smile.

Chapter Eleven

Aristion

482 BCE

The sun had just crested the horizon and the city was bathed in a half-light that signaled morning. I dressed and made my way to Kallian's room, knocking gently on his door.

"Yes," came a muffled reply.

I turned the latch and entered.

"Good morning, I hope you got a good night's sleep—I'm off to check out a number of shops for purchase."

"Just give me a few minutes to get ready and I'll join you!" Kallian replied, rubbing the sleep from his eyes.

"No need. Just take the day to explore," I replied with a smile.

"Are you sure?"

"Yes—just don't get into any trouble."

"I'll try not to!" Kallian replied, grinning sheepishly.

"I'll meet you for dinner in the common room."

Truth be told, I was not sure what measures I'd have to take in order to secure a purchase. It would be better if Kallian was not around to witness it.

~

Since it was early, there were not many people on the street. The quiet roads, usually bustling with activity, were now eerily still. Much of the population was still asleep, recovering from the previous night's festivities.

Walking, I debated on the best option. If we were to gather information, it was important that the shop had the type of foot traffic that yielded information regarding the Persian military and its disposition. To this end, a shop that sold weapons would probably be a good option. Plus, weapons were in Kallian's area of expertise and he would excel in that type of environment.

I noticed a young man walking towards me carrying a basket of bread.

"Excuse me, do you know where I could purchase a sword?" I asked politely.

The handsome youth paused and looked me up and down.

"Yes—if you take the street on the left, just before the gate at the bottom of the hill, you'll see a shop that sells all manner of weapons."

"Much appreciated!" I replied, tossing the lad a coin that he caught deftly with his free hand.

"Thank you, sir," he stammered, grinning from ear to ear.

A few minutes later I found the shop, just as an elderly man opened the door in anticipation of the business the day would bring. He glanced at me and his face lit up with a warm smile.

"Greetings, can I help you?"

"Yes, are you open?"

"Yes—yes!" he replied, beckoning me to follow.

It was then that I observed a wooden peg, beginning just below his left knee. From what I could tell, it did not seem to be a hindrance, as he walked back into the shop with speed and graceful agility. I surmised that he must have had the appendage for a while and was used to it.

He reached the counter, turned and noticed where I was looking.

"I lost it three decades ago during the Scythian campaign," he remarked, completely unbothered. "Are you in the market for a sword, dagger or bow?"

"Not exactly," I replied. "I'm in the market for a shop. Have you considered selling?"

He looked surprised, but then shook his head.

"I'm not ready to put my feet up—or should I say foot," he chuckled. "You can't believe the grief I get about it from my wife. She keeps telling me that I should retire, since I'm obviously on my last leg!"

I let out a belly laugh, but inwardly I groaned. I was not expecting the task to be easy and had already resigned myself to the fact that I may have to visit a number of businesses before finding a willing seller.

"Behrouz, don't be so hasty! At least see what the lad is willing to offer!" a female voice chimed in.

We both turned to see a heavy-set woman, about 50 years of age, standing in a doorway at the back of the shop. She had a sturdy, imposing presence, with broad shoulders and a strong, no-nonsense demeanor. Her graying hair was tied back in a practical braid, revealing a face lined with the marks of age and hard work. Her dark eyes, sharp and perceptive, missed nothing in her surroundings. She wore a simple, earth-toned tunic made of coarse wool, cinched at the waist with a plain, worn leather belt. The sleeves of her tunic were rolled up to her elbows, showing her strong, calloused arms, accustomed to labor. Her feet were clad in sturdy leather sandals, and she had a small cloth pouch hanging from her belt. Her hands, rough and strong, rested on her hips as she surveyed the scene with a look of authority.

"Yasamin, let me handle this!" the man exclaimed, his facing displaying a hint of a scowl.

"You were about to dismiss the man out of hand. At least hear his offer," she replied, walking into the room and taking a seat.

The shopkeeper looked perturbed by the interruption, but she was obviously not going to back down and his face settled in an expression of resignation. It was obvious who wore the *shalvar's* in this relationship! The wife was the person I'd be negotiating with.

"Fine, let's hear it," he replied, looking back at me.

I opened my pack, removed a large purse and tipped the entire contents on the table in front of me.

As the last of the coins spun and came to a standstill, the woman's face lit up and the man let out a breath—a whistle escaping from the gap between two of his upper teeth. The table was now littered in gold *daric's*, the official standard of the Persian Empire. The coin had been in use for over two decades and had been created by Darius I. Not wanting to keep the designs of the defeated Lydian king Croesus , Darius had transitioned away from the Lydian gold stater, minted a new denomination and named it after himself. Although he had passed away two years prior, his son Xerxes I had retained the standard.

The shopkeeper sat back, staring at the pile of gold—a stunned expression on his face.

"YOU WON"T GET A BETTER OFFER. YOU SHOULD TAKE IT!" I said slowly, adding a degree of vrykolakas intonation to my voice as I spoke.

I could feel him resisting the suggestion I was planting in his mind, but the sight of the gold was powerful—adding its own intrinsic power to the weight of my words.

"I think we should take the boy up on his offer," his wife stated, smiling as she spoke. "I've been wanting to move back to Persepolis to be close to my sister—it's time."

The minutes seemed to drag, as he considered my proposal. His face was grim and he appeared to be in the midst of an internal battle, one that was causing his forehead to furrow in concentration. The shop had probably been his entire life since the loss of his leg and it was not an easy decision for him to make—which was understandable.

"OK, I'll sell!" he exclaimed, his face finally relaxing.

"Wonderful—you made the right decision!" I reassured him. "How about we conclude the transaction the day after the festival ends?"

"Yes, that works!" he replied, still looking dazed.

"Excellent!"

A few minutes later I was walking back up the street towards the inn and counting my blessings. I could not believe in my good fortune. The day had barely started and I was already the owner of a shop.

Chapter Twelve

Kallian

481 BCE

A year had passed since their arrival in Sardis, and their endeavors had already borne fruit. The once-quiet shop was now a bustling hub of activity, with a constant stream of customers passing through its doors. Many of these patrons held positions of authority within the Persian military, their presence lending an air of importance to the establishment. The walls of the shop were adorned with finely crafted goods, each piece a testament to the skill and dedication of its artisans.

Aristion had taken the opportunity to befriend a number of high-ranking officials and officers, his keen social skills and sharp wit serving him well in these interactions. He had a way of making people feel at ease, drawing them into conversation with his charm and engaging manner. It was quite remarkable the amount of information that could be gleaned once a person's tongue had been loosened by the application of alcohol. Aristion had become adept at this subtle art, ensuring that the finest wines and spirits were always available for his distinguished guests.

~

Kallian inspected the blade he had just polished, tilting it slightly to catch the light. The polished iron gleamed, reflecting a sharp, mirror-like finish that spoke of his meticulous craftsmanship. He ran a finger along the edge, testing its sharpness, and nodded in satisfaction before placing it gently on the table in front of him. He had to admit, he liked the work and his knowledge of weapons had grown immensely over the past year.

There was a jingle as the bell located above the front door signaled that someone had just entered the premises. He looked up to see Aristion, carrying a large flagon of ale.

"Let's close up for the day and get in some sword practice," he remarked, giving Kallian a warm smile.

"Sounds good to me!"

Kallian had become quite fond of Aristion over the time they had been together. There were still moments in which he missed Eioneus, but with each passing day the pangs he felt in regards to the loss of his friend were gradually fading. He had begun to embrace his new life.

Grabbing his sword and scabbard, he made his way to the door at the rear of the shop—to the room that had been set aside for sword practice. Aristion had insisted that they train every day, explaining that it was essential for Kallian to remain in top form, since it was only a matter of time before he would be required to fight. Just as with a fine sword, it would not do to allow his skill to become "rusty".

Aristion's words echoed in his mind as he entered the practice room, a space sparsely furnished but for a few wooden dummies and targets. The walls were adorned with various weapons, each meticulously maintained, their polished surfaces reflecting the dim light from the oil lamps. Kallian drew his *akīnaka*, feeling the familiar weight of the weapon in his hand.

"How was your day?" Aristion inquired.

"It was quiet—not much to report!"

They walked into the center of the training space and Aristion immediately went into a guard position, which Kallian mirrored.

Aristion was inhumanly fast, the swiftest person Kallian had ever encountered. He was the first opponent who could consistently best him in combat. Initially, this had been a source of great consternation, leaving Kallian questioning his own ability to defend himself. However, over time, he began to see the benefits of having such a skilled adversary. Though he hadn't thought it possible, his skill level had actually increased as a result of their daily sparring sessions.

Aristion was an excellent teacher, combining patience with a relentless drive for perfection. His insights and techniques were invaluable, pushing Kallian beyond his limits and refining his abilities. Kallian was thankful for the time and effort his companion was investing in his training, understanding that each session brought him closer to mastering his craft.

They had only been fighting for a matter of minutes when the doorbell jingled again, signaling the arrival of another customer.

"Damn, I forgot to lock the door," Aristion grumbled. "Do you mind checking to see who it is?"

"Sure," Kallian replied, exiting the room, sword in hand.

Standing in the entrance of the shop were three youths. They looked to be about 20 years of age and were dressed in attire that was typical of Achaemenid Dynasty nobles. Kallian groaned, but still managed to retain a semblance of a smile. He was not in the mood to have to deal with the attitude that was prevalent amongst most men of their political standing—the worst part being that he had to be polite rather than running them through with his sword.

"I'm sorry, we are closed!" Kallian announced, placing his sword on the counter in front of him.

The youth that appeared to be the one in charge, glared at him.

"Not to me," he slurred, obviously drunk.

"My apologies, but we are, even to you—can you come back in the morning?"

"No, you will attend me," the man replied, his lips curling into a sneer. "Don't you know who I am?"

Kallian was already irritated and his ability to treat the men politely was quickly evaporating.

"I don't and neither do I care. Come back tomorrow."

"Insolent boy—this is the nephew of the Satrap," one of the other men snapped.

Kallian felt his hackles rise. Now, he definitely did not want to serve them, given the attitude of unadulterated arrogance they were displaying.

"Bijan, it's OK, we can make time for these gentlemen," Aristion interrupted as he entered the shop, referring to Kallian by the Persian name they had agreed upon.

The youth who had just spoken, glanced at Aristion, his anger dissipating. A sickly smile came over his face.

"That's more like it," he remarked. "At least someone in this establishment knows how to speak to their betters!"

"Go grab some food. I'll take care of the customers." Aristion grimaced, looking at Kallian and motioning towards the door.

Kallian could tell that Aristion was angry. However, unlike Kallian, Aristion was the epitome of self-control when it came to his emotions. Kallian, despite his prowess in combat, was still young and occasionally allowed his feelings to get the better of him. Aristion, on the other hand, maintained a calm, composed demeanor, even in the face of provocation. His ability to remain collected under pressure was something Kallian deeply admired and aspired to emulate.

Aristion's anger was visible only in the slight tightening of his jaw and the intense focus in his eyes. He channeled his emotions into a razor-sharp concentration, a skill honed over years of experience. Kallian recognized this as another lesson to be learned from his mentor—the importance of mastering one's emotions as thoroughly as one masters the blade.

Begrudgingly, he picked up his sword and made his way to the door.

"It's my brother's birthday, and I find myself in the market for a sword," the obnoxious youth declared, placing both hands on the counter to seek a semblance of support in his inebriated state.

"What type of sword do you have in mind?" Aristion responded, his face neutral and his voice steady.

"A *shamshir*—a man's weapon, not like that kid's toy your assistant is carrying," he replied, his tone dripping with condescension. He obviously knew that Kallian was still within earshot and wanted to get in a final jab.

Kallian hesitated in the doorway, seething, his anger almost overwhelming what little remained of his ability to exercise restraint. Oh, how he wished he could turn and run the man through. However, it was not to be. Gritting his teeth, he stormed out of the shop, letting the door slam behind him with a resounding thud.

Chapter Thirteen

Aristion

481 BCE

Later that evening, as we made our way to the bathhouse, my thoughts strayed to Kallian. I felt a growing concern about his altercation with the three nobles. We could not afford to draw negative attention from individuals of their social standing within Persian society.

"How are you doing?" I asked, hoping to gauge his mood.

"Fine—I'm over it," Kallian replied, though his expression betrayed lingering frustration. "People like that annoy the hell out of me."

"Yeah, me too," I said, nodding in agreement. "Just remember to keep your eye on the prize. The intelligence we're gathering is crucial and will more than likely give our country an edge when we have to fight them."

"I know," Kallian agreed, forcing a smile. "I'm eager for that day to come. All this cloak and dagger stuff can be a little vexing, even with the benefits it may yield. Hopefully, I'll get the opportunity to face that son of a whore on the battlefield. I don't think there's anything that would give me more pleasure than using my 'child's toy' to remove his arrogant head!"

"I hope you get the opportunity," I replied, grinning.

A few moments of silence ensued as we continued to walk up the steep main thoroughfare of the upper city. The stone structure of the bathhouse came into view, its grandeur unmistakable even in the fading light of evening. The building was constructed of large, well-fitted stones, their surfaces worn smooth by time and the elements. Tall columns flanked the entrance, adorned with intricate carvings that depicted scenes of nature and mythology, showcasing the artistry of ancient craftsmen.

Breaking the silence, I turned to Kallian. "Can I offer you some advice?" I asked.

"Yes," Kallian responded, begrudgingly.

"You are a masterful fighter, one of the best I've ever met. However, unless you can master your emotions, they'll end up getting the better of you. It's not something we can afford in our current situation."

"I know," Kallian grimaced, frustration evident in his voice.

"Even in combat, emotional restraint is essential. As skilled as you are, if you lose control, you could end up making a fatal mistake. Many good fighters have lost their lives because of it."

Kallian nodded in agreement but remained silent, so I continued.

"One of the tactics used by a skilled fighter when facing an opponent who is close to them in ability, or better, is to try and evoke an emotional response—such as anger. If you can cause them to lose control, they will invariably take risks and leave openings that you can exploit. It can tip the balance of a fight."

I now had his complete attention, so I took a breath and made eye contact.

"A successful engagement is fought not only with the sword but also with the mind. This applies to both individual combat and situations where you are leading others into battle. Master your mind, and it will give you an upper hand over most opponents—especially given your technical ability."

"Yes, I get it," Kallian replied earnestly. "How do I train my mind like you're saying?"

"We'll work on it together. When we spar tomorrow, we can do an exercise that should help."

"I'd like that, thank you!"

"You probably won't be thanking me once we begin," I laughed, a mischievous glint in my eyes as I spoke.

"Oh great—I can't wait," Kallian muttered, feigning nervousness before breaking into a grin.

~

Kallian walked over to the door of the shop and slid the bolt into place. A day had passed since our conversation, and he was excited for the lesson that was about to begin.

"Let's do it!" he exclaimed, turning to me.

I smiled and walked into the back room, gesturing with my head for him to follow. He had no idea what was in store for him.

We warmed up for a few minutes, moving through a series of standard sword forms—as we cut, thrust, and parried, the swords ringing as they clashed.

Kallian began to quicken his pace, which I matched effortlessly. I generally exercised a degree of restraint when fighting humans, careful not to reveal the full extent of my abilities. If I moved with the speed of a vrykolakas, I could end the fight in an instant. Kallian wouldn't stand a chance. All he would see would be a blur of motion before my sword was at his throat. However, he was merely mortal, and my goal was to train him to fight others like himself, not someone like me.

Circling me, his eyes locked on mine, his brows furrowed in concentration. I dropped the tip of my sword, deliberately leaving an opening. He took it without a second's hesitation, stepping forward swiftly and lunging at me.

I swept my sword up, parrying his blade, and then lashed out with my foot. He instinctively pivoted to the right in a half-circle, narrowly avoiding my kick. Continuing his spin, he brought his sword around in a wide arc. Our swords met with a loud clash of iron against iron, the force of the impact resonating through the air.

The fight went on, our blades continuing to ring out as they clashed with every swing, slash, and parry—in an intricate dance of swordsmanship. Each movement was precise and calculated, a testament to Kallian's growing skill and my practiced expertise.

Kallian was now warmed up, and it was time for the actual lesson to begin. As he took a step back, I engaged a fraction of my vrykolakas speed and moved in. Quicker than a viper snapping at a rodent, I sidestepped his sword, slipped within his guard, and slapped him hard across the face, spinning away as I did so.

Kallian swung wildly in response, his sword missing my chest by a wide margin. Before his *akīnaka* had even completed its arc, I spun back in and repeated the process. There was a loud slap as my palm made contact with his face for a second time. I then leapt back, effortlessly out of range before he had a chance to respond.

"Is that the best you've got, or do you want me to keep slapping you like a petulant child?" I chided, my lips curling into a smirk.

"DAMN YOU TO HELL!" he shouted.

The words had barely passed his lips before I moved in and slapped him again—to which he responded with a series of wild swings, all poise and artistry gone from his movements.

"KALLIAN! Control your anger!" I shouted.

He glared at me as I spoke, his face flushed red. I couldn't tell if it was from rage or the fact that I had been hitting him.

"Stop for a second," I commanded. "Take a deep breath and find your center. When you fight, don't let your opponent's words affect you. Be deaf to them—as if they are water flowing off a duck's back. Focus only on their eyes and body movements. Look for any tells they might give that signal their next move."

Kallian reined in his emotions and took a deep breath. He nodded at me, his face relaxing, and his eyes displaying a glint of fierce determination. He was a quick learner.

"You are fast," he declared, wiping the sweat from his brow with his free hand. "I don't think I've ever seen anyone move that quickly!"

"All the more reason for you to remain calm and keep your emotions in check. It's the only way you'll have a chance to beat a skilled opponent like me!" I replied, giving him a smile of encouragement.

"Let's continue!" Kallian responded eagerly, moving his sword into a front guard position, his blade held vertically in front of his face.

"Alright—but I'm not going to use my sword," I said, placing my *shamshir* aside. Kallian's eyes widened in shock for a moment, clearly taken aback by my decision.

"You're not going to use your sword?" he asked, disbelief mingling with curiosity.

"Exactly. Are you ready?" I replied, my tone firm and unwavering.

"Yes!" he affirmed, his initial surprise quickly replaced by a steely determination.

Over the course of the next hour, I continued to strike and cajole him. Although I could see a flicker of frustration on his face each time I slapped him, he managed to remain calm and focused. Despite my best efforts, I could not provoke the anger I had seen at the beginning of the exercise. His composure and determination held firm, a testament to his growing control and resilience.

"Much better!" I commended, shifting my weight to my left foot in preparation for my next attack.

He must have noticed the slight alteration in my stance because he instantly brought the hilt of his *akīnaka* up above his head, angling the blade down to protect the right side of his face. My hand stopped a hair's breadth from the sharp edge of his weapon. Without hesitation, he kneed me in the stomach. As I doubled over, a look of grim satisfaction spread across his face.

"Finally!" he exclaimed, his mouth breaking into a grin.

I came back to full height and smiled.

"Excellent!"

His face was now a picture of pure satisfaction, the light from the lanterns reflecting off the beads of perspiration running down his forehead and into his eyes. I took in the striking figure standing before me, his chiseled features framed by long, black curly hair, still wet from the intense training we had just endured.

Our eyes met, and the room descended into silence. It was as if time had come to a standstill, with neither of us able, or wanting, to break the intense connection we were feeling. I leaned in, and our lips touched. His mouth opened to receive mine, and I felt one of his hands slide around the back of my head while the other wrapped around my back. He pulled me close, locking us in an embrace. As we kissed, mouths open and tongues entwined, I completely lost myself in the passion of our mutual attraction.

Eventually, I broke contact and stepped back, still gazing into his eyes. What had I gotten myself into?

~

Later that evening, as we made our way to the bathhouse, we walked in silence. I was lost in thought, reflecting on my feelings for Kallian. I had grown to care deeply for him, and I realized my feelings had evolved past simple affection into love. I wasn't sure when it had happened, but the kiss had confirmed it.

It had been a long time since I had felt this way, and it brought with it a pang of fear. I had already experienced the intense pain of losing my first lover, which had left me hesitant to open myself up to the possibility of it happening again. Kallian was mortal, and I was destined to outlive him. His lifespan would be over in the blink of an eye compared to that of a vrykolakas.

Still in turmoil, I thought about our mission. It had to take priority over my personal life, and pursuing an intimate relationship might put it at risk. If it came down to it, I might have to make a hard decision, one that could result in his death.

As we stripped off, I glanced in Kallian's direction just as he unceremoniously dropped the last article of his clothing to the marble floor. With his back turned to me, I took the opportunity to appreciate the beautifully contoured muscles of his back, legs, and well-developed glutes. The soft light of the bathhouse accentuated his physique, each muscle defined and prominent. He then turned, and the semi-aroused state of his manhood became evident. In fact, it was hard to miss.

Our eyes met, and I let out a deep sigh. Restraining myself was going to be incredibly difficult—even more so than the training I had undergone with Megareus to control my insatiable appetite for blood. The intensity of my feelings for Kallian was an entirely new challenge for me—testing my self-control in ways I had never anticipated.

His gaze held a mixture of curiosity and something deeper, making it even more difficult to maintain my composure. I could feel the magnetic pull between us, a powerful force that was almost impossible to resist. He was quickly becoming a test of my willpower and a constant reminder of the boundaries I needed to maintain to protect the integrity of our mission. I couldn't help but wonder how I would navigate this delicate balance.

Chapter Fourteen

Aristion

481 BCE

I marveled at my own restraint as I recalled the previous night's shared bath with Kallian. Despite the overwhelming desire I felt for him, I had succeeded in keeping my composure. However, my reticence to engage further or discuss the intense moment we had shared seemed to have left him perplexed, a sentiment clearly reflected in his questioning gaze. I knew that we would need to address the matter once I had a chance to sort through my own feelings.

As morning dawned, I found solace in the prospect of the day's mission. Immersing myself in the task at hand provided a welcome distraction from the emotional whirlwind I was navigating.

A few days prior I had uncovered some information regarding the order of Zoroastrian Warrior Clerics. They had had established a new garrison complex, or *khāné Atash Aršti* and it was located in a building attached to the city's main *ataskada*—a place of worship for those of the Zoroastrian faith. The name *khāné Atash Aršti* roughly translates to "House of the Burning Spear". More precisely, the word *atash* embodies the Zoroastrian concept of holy fire, sometimes described in abstract terms such as "*burning and unburning fire*" or "*visible and invisible fire*".

Given the fact that the order was establishing a presence in Sardis, the garrison would definitely include at least one *mágos*—a practitioner of magic and the only real threat to my kind. Not only could they detect a vrykolakas when they came within a couple of cart lengths of one, they also had the power to paralyze and bind a vrykolakas using sorcery.

Although the Greeks had bankrolled my relocation to Sardis, in return for information regarding the disposition of the Persian military and advance warnings of invasion, it was not my primary mission. Megareus, my master, and the vrykolakas council had given me the task of eliminating the Achaemenid dynasty of Persia's ability to use magic. The *mágos* could not be allowed to exist—they had to go.

~

Despite the early hour, the streets bustled with activity. Shoppers meandered among the vibrant market stalls, their colorful displays of spices, fabrics, and trinkets drawing the eye. The air was filled with the enticing aromas of freshly baked bread and exotic spices, mingling with the sounds of vendors calling out their wares.

A steady stream of visitors flowed in and out of the temple, their footsteps echoing against the ancient stone walls. Some were pilgrims, their faces marked with reverence, while others were locals going about their daily rituals. The temple's grandeur, with its towering columns and intricate carvings, stood as a testament to the city's rich history and spiritual significance.

I kept my gaze low, appearing to be lost in my own world, but in reality, I was acutely aware of my surroundings. My eyes flickered toward the building of the Zoroastrian Warrior Clerics, noting every movement and detail.

Eventually, I saw two men exit the order's building. They were dressed in cleric livery, their robes pristine and marked with the symbols of their order. *Shamshirs* hung at their hips, a clear indication of their combat prowess. They walked with purpose, their expressions stern and focused.

I contemplated following them but decided to wait. It would be better to target a single cleric, one who could be isolated without drawing attention. Patience was crucial; a single misstep could jeopardize the entire mission. I settled back, feigning indifference, while my mind remained sharp and alert, ready for the opportunity to strike.

My patience was soon rewarded as a lone cleric stepped out of the doorway and began to saunter around the market, obviously looking for something to purchase. He stopped by a stall selling bread and proffered coin to its attendant, in return for a freshly baked loaf.

I rose to my feet and moved to intercept him before he had a chance to make his way back to the building that housed the order.

“Please sir, can you spare some coin?” I pleaded, proffering the bowl in my outstretched hand.

“Get out of my way—scum!” he spluttered; his mouth full of bread. “I don’t have time for—.”

“STOP!” I hissed, using the full extent of my vrykolakas power to mesmerize my target.

Instantly, his mouth snapped shut, cutting off whatever he was about to say. He stood before me, motionless, his glazed eyes signaling that he was now under my complete control. At this moment, the man would do anything I asked of him.

I grinned, satisfied that everything was going according to plan.

“FOLLOW ME!”

I retraced my steps down the bustling street, the sounds of vendors hawking their wares fading behind me as I slipped into a narrow alleyway. Pausing close to the entrance, I glanced back, ensuring I was concealed from view. He stood several paces away from me, his back turned to the teeming thoroughfare. In the seclusion of the alley, I prepared myself for the interrogation I was about to engage in.

“HOW MANY CLERICS ARE LOCATED IN SARDIS?”

“Fifty,” he replied, his tone neutral and without inflection.

“HOW MANY MAGOS ARE LOCATED IN SARDIS?”

“Three.”

“HOW MANY MAGOS ARE IN YOUR ORDER?”

“Twelve.”

“DO ANY OF THE MAGOS IN SARDIS VENTURE OUT WITHOUT ARMED GUARDS?”

“Yes.”

"ELABORATE!"

"Hashem goes to The Inn of the Seven Horses most evenings."

With a sense of grim satisfaction, I smiled. He had giving me exactly I needed.

After ordering the cleric to forget our meeting, I dismissed him and began to make my way back to the shop, formulating a plan of action as I walked.

This week would herald my most daring endeavor yet—the assassination of a *mágos*. Their elimination was crucial to crippling the Achaemenid dynasty's use of magic. Each step I took echoed my resolve, the weight of the task settling heavily on my shoulders.

Chapter Fifteen

Kallian

481 BCE

The young man who had just purchased a sword from Kallian exited the shop with a spring in his step, the weight of his new weapon balanced carefully in his hands. He was clearly eager to test it out, his eyes alight with excitement. As he stepped onto the bustling street, his attention was so focused on the finely crafted blade that he nearly collided with Aristion, who was returning from his errands.

Aristion, laden with various parcels and supplies, deftly sidestepped the young man at the last moment. The near-collision caused the young man to look up, his face flushing with embarrassment. "Sorry, sir," he mumbled, his enthusiasm momentarily dampened.

Aristion, ever the gracious one, gave a nod of acknowledgment and a faint smile. "No harm done," he said smoothly, his keen eyes quickly assessing the young man and the sword he carried

As Aristion entered, he found Kallian tidying up the counter, clearly satisfied with the sale. The shop was bathed in the warm morning light filtering through the windows, casting a soft glow on the array of finely crafted weapons and armor.

"Good morning, I hope you slept well," Aristion remarked, setting his parcels down on a nearby table.

"Yes, once I finally managed to fall asleep!" Kallian replied with a forced smile.

In truth, he had not slept at all. He had spent most of the night wide awake, his mind racing with thoughts about the previous evening's events. Kallian had been feeling an intense attraction toward Aristion almost since their arrival in Sardis. However, he had suppressed those feelings, never even considering the possibility that they might be reciprocated.

The kiss had come as a complete surprise, unleashing the full extent of his desire for his friend and mentor. However, Aristion had been distant since it happened. Even at the baths, where Kallian's longing had been unmistakable, Aristion had not acted upon it. The mixed messages had left him conflicted and in a state of emotional turmoil. As much as he cared for Aristion, the man's behavior was insufferable!

The flickering lanterns from the previous night's vigil still hung in the corners, casting gentle shadows on the walls. Kallian stole a glance at Aristion, who was now unpacking the parcels with his usual composed efficiency. Yet, there was a subtle warmth in his eyes when he occasionally glanced at Kallian, hinting at deeper feelings.

Kallian couldn't help but replay the kiss in his mind, the way their lips had met with such unexpected intensity. It had confirmed everything he had tried to ignore—the irresistible attraction, the unspoken connection. Now, standing in the same room with Aristion, he felt a mixture of excitement and apprehension. The air between them seemed charged with unspoken possibilities.

Aristion, seemingly oblivious to Kallian's inner turmoil, continued to arrange the new supplies with practiced efficiency. The tension in the room was palpable, a quiet hum of unspoken emotions hanging in the air.

"Where did you go?" Kallian inquired.

"To gather intelligence on the Zoroastrian Warrior Clerics and their new chapter house."

"Did it go well?"

"Yes," and after a brief pause, added, "I was thinking—why don't you take a day to yourself, I'm more than happy to man the shop."

"Are you sure?"

"Yes! I'm actually in the mood for some game this evening. Are you down for a little hunting?"

Kallian's eyes lit up at this. There was nothing he liked to do more than hunt. The thrill of tracking his prey, the adrenaline rush of the chase, and the satisfaction of a successful capture or kill—these were experiences that resonated deeply within him. For him, hunting was not just a pastime; it was a passion.

~

Two hours later, Kallian was lying on his stomach, his bow beside him. From his vantage point, he had a clear view of a small clearing nestled near the center of the wooded area, close to the banks of the Pactolus at the base of Mount Tmolus. The area was rich in vegetation and teeming with wildlife. A gentle breeze carried the fragrance of spring flowers, accompanied by the melodious chirping of countless birds. It was a scene of serene beauty.

Kallian's thoughts strayed to Aristion, to the kiss, but were quickly interrupted by the sudden appearance of three rabbits in the clearing. They were nibbling on the lush grass typical of the riverbank area. Swiftly, he picked up his bow and assumed a kneeling position, being careful to avoid disturbing the surrounding foliage. Holding his weapon horizontally, he strung an arrow, pulled back the bowstring, and sighted on the closest rabbit. With a steady exhale, he released the arrow. It struck the small animal, causing it to twitch briefly before lying still. Sensing the danger, the other rabbits bolted into the nearby trees.

Satisfied with his successful hunt, Kallian rose to his feet and retrieved the warm, furry bundle. He placed it carefully into the large leather bag slung over his shoulder, ensuring it was secure.

With his hunting concluded sooner than expected and many hours of daylight to spare, Kallian was not ready to head home. After a brief moment of contemplation, he decided on a swim in the Pactolus River. As much as he enjoyed the baths, the allure of swimming in a river was irresistible.

The thought of the cool, flowing water brought a smile to his face. It reminded him of his time at the *agōgē*, a period in his life that he often reflected upon. Life seemed so uncomplicated back then.

Standing on an outcropping of rock overlooking the river, Kallian shed his garments and dove in. The water was brisk, almost stealing his breath, but it cleansed his mind of the emotional turmoil he had endured over the past day. It brought him into the present moment, where he finally found peace. Surfacing, he floated on his back, the water cradling him like a loving embrace.

Kallian swam leisurely for a while, until the chill of the water began to penetrate, causing him to shiver. Making his way to the bank, he emerged from the river and climbed onto the sun-warmed rock where he had left his clothes. Stretching out, he allowed the sun's rays to envelop him, while droplets of water, glistening like stars, cascaded from his naked form onto the stone beneath him.

"What do we have here?" a voice interrupted the tranquility, dripping with condescension, shattering the silence.

Kallian opened his eyes and peered up, shielding them with his hand from the glare of the sun. Three men, adorned in the attire of Persian nobility, sat astride white horses. He sighed as he recognized them—the same youths who had visited the shop a few days prior.

"Well, if it isn't the little runt from the shop!" the man added, his tone dripping with malevolence as he dismounted.

Kallian realized trouble was brewing. If he couldn't defuse the tension, he might be forced to defend himself. He glanced at his sword but refrained from touching it, knowing that any aggressive move would only escalate the situation.

"Hello, gentlemen. How may I assist you?" he inquired calmly, aiming for deference.

The leader sneered in reply, his gaze fixed on Kallian, while the others mirrored his actions and dismounted. "I believe it's time we taught the little runt some manners."

In unison, the three men drew their *shamshirs* and advanced toward him.

The possibility of avoiding conflict evaporated like a drop of water hitting a hot skillet. Kallian seized his sword, and within two heartbeats, it was unsheathed, and he was on his feet, facing them.

"You can't handle me by yourself—you need your friends to help you?" Kallian growled, the politeness gone from his voice.

The man paused, raising one hand to signal the others to stop. He regarded Kallian thoughtfully for a few seconds.

"The runt is actually correct—wonders never cease!" he finally declared. "I was trained by a grand master and can beat this peasant with one arm tied behind my back!"

His two friends stepped back, giving him space. He advanced again, this time alone.

Kallian dropped into a guard position as the pride of Persian nobility unleashed a quick flurry of sword swings that passed over his head and down his torso, before coming to a standstill, matching Kallian's ready stance. If it was meant to intimidate him, he was unimpressed. The man's overconfidence and arrogant showmanship were apparent, but they would be his undoing.

Casually closing the distance, Kallian's opponent lunged with a diagonal slicing arc of his *shamshir*, which he parried with ease, sweeping the other weapon aside.

The fight continued, but despite the noble's efforts, he couldn't land a blow. Kallian intercepted and parried every strike effortlessly. His opponent's training by a grandmaster was evident, but he was no match for Kallian's years of rigorous training at the *agōgē*.

"Why don't you attack?" the man shouted, sweat dripping from his brow, spittle falling from his lips—his face a picture of unbridled anger.

Truth be told, Kallian was conflicted. During their clash, he ran through various scenarios in his head. If he defeated the noble without killing him, the man might target the shop, jeopardizing their mission. This left two options: kill or be killed. He felt like Odysseus navigating between Scylla and Charybdis in the Strait of Messina. Regardless of his choice, the outcome would be dire.

The sun beat down on them, casting harsh shadows and highlighting the intensity of the moment. The air was thick with the scent of sweat and dust, the clash of iron ringing out sharply.

Finally reaching a decision, Kallian sprinted forward, pivoting as he moved and bringing his sword around in a swift arc. His opponent blocked it and attempted a thrust to Kallian's stomach, which he sidestepped. Instantly, Kallian moved within the man's guard, elbowing him in the nose, causing the man to stagger back. With his foe wide open, Kallian lunged forward and thrust his *xiphos* directly into the man's chest.

The noble's eyes widened in shock as he fell to his knees, his breath escaping in a pained gasp. Kallian stood over him, his heart pounding, knowing that he had chosen the path that would best protect their mission, even if it weighed heavily on his conscience. The sun cast long shadows over the scene, highlighting the gravity of the moment as the noble's life ebbed away.

As Kallian withdrew his sword, the man looked down, and blood began to expand outward from the location where he had just been impaled. There was still a look of shock on his face, which soon turned to horror as the realization of what had just happened set in.

"Not bad for a runt with a child's toy," Kallian muttered, meeting the man's eyes for the last time before he collapsed to the ground. Blood spread on the dirt beneath him, and he let out a final breath, becoming still. His eyes remained open but were now devoid of life, reflecting the brutal finality of their confrontation.

The two companions, momentarily stunned by the unexpected turn of events, burst into motion. They ran at Kallian, swords swinging. He effortlessly parried the blade of the first to reach him, then delivered a swift kick to the stomach, causing the man to grunt with pain and fall onto his back. Kallian then met the blade of the second combatant as it arced towards his chest.

The sound from the initial clash of blades still hung in the air as Kallian launched into an offensive series of well-practiced moves. The first and second strikes were blocked, his enemy swinging wildly in a desperate attempt to defend himself. The third strike sliced open his throat, causing the man to drop his sword and try to staunch the blood spraying from the wound with both hands. Kallian seized the opportunity to finish him off with a quick thrust to the heart.

The entire fight had taken place within a matter of a few breaths, and the surviving combatant—who was still on the ground—was now scrabbling backward. Kallian began to walk towards him. There was a look of sheer terror on the face of the fallen man as he turned onto all fours and launched himself to his feet, not even bothering to pick up his fallen sword. With adrenaline pumping through his veins, the man ran for his horse and made it into the saddle in a single leap.

As the beast bolted, Kallian briefly considered his options before walking over to his bow. Picking it up, he notched an arrow, drew back, sighted, and let it fly. The arrow caught the man squarely between the shoulder blades. However, the horse continued to run as the figure slumped over in the saddle and then, almost in slow motion, gradually toppled sideways and fell to the ground.

Kallian placed his bow on the ground, picked up his sword, and strolled over to where the man lay. He was still alive and coughing up blood.

"Please—please, spare me!" he gurgled, as he looked up at Kallian.
"You won't get any mercy from me," Kallian replied, expressionless, before slicing the man's throat with the tip of his sword."

He surveyed the carnage that surrounded him. It had been unavoidable—but they had brought it upon themselves.

Kallian knelt next to the man lying at his feet and began to rifle through the small pack that had been slung diagonally across one of his shoulders. He found a coin purse, which he transferred to his own pack. When the bodies were found, the authorities would probably presume that the men had been robbed and killed by bandits. He then picked up the man's sword and threw it as far as he could into the river.

After repeating the process with the other men, Kallian walked over to the two remaining horses. They were happily munching on some tufts of grass, their ears twitching lazily, as if they did not have a care in the world. He approached them quietly, the soft rustling of his footsteps barely disturbing their peaceful grazing.

With a firm slap on each rump, the horses started in alarm, their heads jerking up as they bolted. Their hooves thundered against the ground, kicking up small clouds of dust as they fled. Kallian watched them, the sunlight glinting off their sleek coats, until they disappeared from sight behind a small rise located between a copse of trees and the banks of the river Pactolus. Finally, after a deep breath, the tension slowly ebbed from his body as the serene landscape reasserted itself.

Satisfied, he got dressed, collected his belongings and mounted. With one final glance over his shoulder, Kallian gave the reins a brief shake and his horse surged into motion.

As he rode, Kallian felt a gentle breeze, bearing the floral scent of spring, caress his face. The fragrance was in stark contrast to the violence that had just transpired. What was he going to tell Aristion? One thing was for sure: Aristion was not going to be happy. Given the status of the nobles he had just killed, the entire city would probably end up in an uproar, and its garrison would likely be mobilized to locate the man or men responsible for killing the beloved son of the Satrap.

Chapter Sixteen

Aristion

481 BCE

The Persian officer, middling in years, burst into laughter as I delivered the punch line of a joke about a donkey, a commoner and a king, attempting to enter *Jannat*, the Zoroastrian idea of paradise or heaven.

"Another—another," the man chortled, taking a swig of ale from the mug on the table in front of him.

"OK, one more—and then I'm out," I replied, grinning.

The man was positively gleeful. I was not sure if it was due to the awful jokes I'd been imparting, or from the sheer magnitude of alcohol we had consumed over the course of the past two hours.

After a few seconds of thought, I settled on my final joke and proceeded.

"One day the King invited Mahmoud to his palace for dinner. The royal chef had prepared, among other things, a cabbage recipe for the occasion.

After the dinner, the King asked, 'How did you like the cabbage?'

'It was very delicious,' complimented Mahmoud.

'I thought it tasted awful,' said the King.

'You're right,' added Mahmoud, 'it was very bland.'

'But you just said it tasted delicious,' the King noted.

'Ah, but I'm the servant of His Majesty, not of the cabbage,' he replied."

I sat back, smiling, as the man roared with laughter. Considering that the only thing funny about the joke was how bad it was, I never had to work that hard to keep the man entertained.

"Well, my friend, I better get going. My wife will kill me if I come home too drunk!" he remarked, as his guffaws finally subsided.

He got to his feet, gave me a friendly slap on the back and begun to buckle on the scabbard that held his *Shamshir*.

The doorbell jingled and Kallian walked in, a bow and pack slung over his back. He smiled warmly at us, in greeting.

"Ghazi, it's great to see you again!" he exclaimed.

"You too, lad!" the old soldier boomed. "Your partner in crime has been keeping me entertained—but it's well past time for me to head off!"

With a final wave, he exited the shop.

"Did you glean anything useful from him today? Kallian queried.

"Not much—besides the fact that a Persian *hazarabam* will be arriving in a few weeks. He's not sure why," I replied, using the Persian term for one of their regiments, a formidable unit composed of a thousand elite soldiers, each trained to perfection and equipped with the finest weapons and armor.

"I guess we will need to determine its mission?" Kallian speculated, as he laid his pack on the table.

"Yes, it shouldn't be hard. There are a lot of loose tongues in this city!" I responded, as I quizzically lifted the flap of Kallian's pack and beamed in response to its contents.

"Excellent—it looks like we'll be eating rabbit for dinner!"

Kallian gave me a brief smile that looked somewhat forced, pulled out a chair and sat, his demeanor becoming serious.

"Dinner can wait. We need to talk."

"What's up?"

He paused, as if he was struggling to find the right words.

"You know the three nobles that came into the shop the other day—the ones that were insulting me?"

"Yes."

"Well—I ran into them when I was out hunting."

The moment he spoke, a shiver ran down my spine, and an ominous weight settled in the pit of my stomach.

"And?" I managed to utter, my voice barely above a whisper, as I motioned for him to continue."

"I killed them," he responded, his face dead pan and expressionless.

"Well—shit!" I blurted out. They were the only words that readily came to mind. "Damnation! This is going to make our life difficult!"

He then elaborated on the events that unfolded, detailing how he orchestrated the scene to make it appear as though the men fell victim to a bandit attack. As he spoke, it became evident that Kallian had carefully weighed his options and ultimately made the most prudent decision.

Listening to his account, I couldn't help but feel a sense of resignation wash over me. However, despite the grim reality of the situation, it was clear that Kallian had acted in the best interest of our mission.

"I was concerned that you'd be angry?"

"No—It was a difficult situation. You handled it well. I would have probably done exactly the same thing!" I replied, giving him an encouraging smile and tousling his long black hair. "How do you feel?"

"Better, now that we've talked," he grinned. "Was it your first kill?"

"Yes."

"And?"

"Honestly, I can't think of anyone more deserving of meeting his end at the tip of my blade," he replied, smirking.

"True!" I responded, nodding my head in agreement. "Well, the deed is done and we are simply going to have to deal with the possible consequences. In the meantime, I'm famished. Let's go cook that rabbit of yours!"

Chapter Seventeen

Aristion

481 BCE

Two days had passed since Kallian's hunting excursion. The city, like they expected, was in an uproar. The three bodies had been discovered the following morning and since then, there had been a constant stream of armed patrols passing through the city gates. Fortunately, Kallian's misdirection had worked and the Satrap had assumed that bandits were responsible for the death of his nephew.

The turn of events had resulted in a reevaluation of my plans. Reluctantly, my mission to assassinate Hashem, the *mágos*, was now on hold, until things calmed down. Instead, I busied myself in the shop—cleaning and creating an inventory of the weapons.

Kallian appeared in the doorway with a flagon of ale and two mugs. "Would you like to join me for a drink?"

"Sure," I replied, smiling and putting the sword down. "I'm just about done anyway."

Kallian pulled over a stool, sat down next to me and poured.

"I'm relieved that they believe it was bandits," he remarked. "I was concerned that it would end up jeopardizing our mission."

"You made the right call," I replied, assuring him and meeting his eyes. "If you had left them alive, they would have made trouble for us."

"Agreed!"

We drank in silence for a few minutes. Occasionally, I caught him looking at me furtively out of the corner of my eye. He seemed to have something on his mind but was hesitant to speak. I knew what it was.

"Kallian, about the kiss..."

When my voice broke the silence, he had been gazing into his mug, swilling its contents around and lost in thought. However, the moment I spoke, he turned to me, his attention rapt.

"Yes, I wanted to talk to you about that," he responded, a look of relief evident on his face.

"I apologize for being so distant—I've just had a lot on my mind." "I know," he replied, a hopeful look in his eyes.

"It must be obvious by now how much I care about you," I continued. "However, I'm not sure if it's a good idea if we pursue an intimate relationship."

Kallian looked crestfallen. Instantly, I felt a tightening in my chest. I was obviously causing him pain and it was making the decision I had come to, even tougher.

"Why?"

I paused, debating how to proceed.

"Our mission has to take priority. It's essential that we do not engage in anything that would affect it, as much as we would like to follow our feelings."

"I don't understand—how would it risk our mission?" he responded, obviously perplexed.

This was turning out to be even more difficult than expected. There was a raging turmoil of conflicting emotions running through my veins and I had to restrain myself from embracing him. Instead, I took a deep breath, regained control and continued.

"We can't allow ourselves to become too attached. Things may transpire that will require a quick decision, one that could place us in danger. When such a moment comes, I need to be able to act without hesitation," I relayed, my voice firm, but gentle. "I don't want my feelings for you to prevent me from doing what needs to be done."

Kallian sat there in silence as I spoke, his face reflecting the same turbulent emotions I was experiencing. Truth be told, I wasn't sure if I was being entirely honest with him or even with myself. In reality, a significant part of me was simply afraid of forming an attachment, especially to someone who was mortal.

His eyes bore into mine, a mixture of hurt and understanding swirling within them. The flickering candlelight cast soft shadows on his face, highlighting the tension etched in his features. The silence between us grew heavy, laden with unspoken words and unshed tears.

Unable to bear the pained expression on his face any longer, I let out a big sigh, leaned back, and closed my eyes. The weight of my own words pressed down on me, a stark reminder of the walls I was building around my heart.

Without so much as another word, Kallian got up and left the room. The sound of his footsteps echoed in the quiet space, a stark contrast to the cacophony of emotions raging within me. As the door closed behind him, the room felt colder, emptier. I opened my eyes and stared at the spot where he had just been, feeling a hollow ache in my chest.

Chapter Eighteen

Aristion

481 BCE

Summer was uneventful and passed quickly. A few weeks after the death of the Satrap's nephew, the hunting parties were finally been recalled. They had discovered a group of marauders in the foothills of Mount Tmolus and eradicated them to the man. It was the perfect outcome; with no survivors to question, the authorities simply assumed that the bandits had been the culprits.

It was now late autumn, and Sardis was in the midst of another festival, *Ayathrem Gahanbar—'bringing home the herds.'* The city had donned its most vibrant attire, embracing the festive spirit with open arms. The chill of the season was countered by the warmth of communal joy, as people from all walks of life converged in the streets to partake in the celebrations.

The festival marked a significant time in the agrarian calendar, a moment to honor the return of the herds from their summer pastures. It was a tradition steeped in history, symbolizing the cycle of life and the community's connection to the land. The air was thick with the mingling scents of roasted meats, spiced wine, and fresh bread, a sensory feast that invited all to indulge.

The city streets were bursting at the seams with festivalgoers, as I wove my way to the Zoroastrian Warrior Clerics base of operation, next to the *ataskada.* Since everything had calmed down in regards to the murder of the young men, the timing was perfect time for me to complete my mission. Hashem, the *mágos*, was going to die.

I sat and waited, begging bowl in hand, my attention fixed on the door of the building next to the temple. Time passed, and I began to feel a pang of doubt as the sun commenced its slow descent behind the rooftop of a nearby building. What if the information I had gleaned from the warrior cleric earlier that year was no longer accurate? Hopefully, the *mágos* still made his daily visit to The Inn of the Seven Horses.

However, my concern was soon dispelled when a man exited the building. He appeared to be approximately 50 years of age, his face marked by a long, scraggly gray beard that ran halfway down his chest. He was clothed in the typical Sasanian dress of the warrior clerics—loose-fitting trousers, boots, and a knee-length tunic bound with a leather belt. Unlike the regular warrior cleric's tunic, his was differentiated by three stripes that ran vertically down its center: one of gold and two of blue. This marked him as a member of the Zoroastrian *mágos*.

I got to my feet and began to follow him at a distance, taking advantage of the vast number of people in Sardis for the festival. I seamlessly merged into the crowd, using their collective motion to shield myself from any unwanted attention.

Unlike the majority of members of the order of Zoroastrian Warrior Clerics, *mágos* had the ability to withstand mind-control. Due to this, I did not have the option of simply walking over to him and ordering him to follow me.

The ability to withstand mesmerization was just one of the many formidable powers of a *mágos*. However, it was far from the most dangerous. Their magical prowess extended to restraining a vrykolakas from a distance. If a *mágos* managed to get within a cart-length and had enough time to weave their enchantments, I would be rendered paralyzed and at their mercy. This potential vulnerability was why the warrior arm of the clerical order was established—not only to protect the *mágos* but also to engage and distract a vrykolakas, buying the *mágos* the precious moments needed to cast their immobilization spells.

We were now almost at the inn, and Hashem's chosen route had not provided a suitable ambush site for later that evening. He was keeping to the main city thoroughfares and there were too many people. I groaned in frustration and was beginning to contemplate a different approach, when he took a sudden turn to the right and entered a narrow ally. It was a shortcut, one that halved the remaining distance to the inn. I sighed with relief. His choice of route would end up being the death of him.

I continued to follow, until he reached the door of the establishment. From what I could tell, the place was packed. Many of its inebriated patrons had spilled out onto the street and Hashem had to wait patiently for a group to exit, before entering.

Satisfied, I doubled back and ascended a long flight of steps nestled in the shadows. The worn stone steps yielded no sound underfoot as I climbed. Halfway up, I found myself at a junction between the two exits of the alley. Darkness enveloped the narrow passage, broken only by the dim glow of distant street lamps. To my right, a squat building cast a looming silhouette against the night sky, offering ample cover for an ambush. With practiced agility, I scaled the side of the structure, feeling the rough texture of the brick against my palms as I positioned myself on the flat roof. From this vantage point, I had a clear view of the alley entrance below, just a stone's throw away from the bustling inn.

Hunkering down in the shadows, I resigned myself to a long wait. The night stretched out before me, the darkness illuminated only by the occasional flicker of lamplight. I knew Hashem would likely linger at the inn well into the evening, immersed in whatever revelry awaited him within those walls. With patience as my sole companion, I settled in as comfortably as possible, all the while feeling the thrill of anticipation pulsating through my veins in anticipation of the impending encounter.

Many hours passed, and the foot traffic through the alley began to dissipate. Even at the height of the evening, it had not been particularly busy, with most people keeping to the well-lit streets of the city.

Eventually, I spotted Hashem. He was obviously inebriated, his gait clumsy as he struggled to walk in a straight line. He stopped, lifted his tunic, and leaned against the side of a building, one hand on its wall. I could hear the trickle of water as he relieved himself.

Business done, Hashem continued down the alley and finally reached the top of the steps. He was now directly below me. I took a breath, leapt, and landed in a crouch behind him. Even when my feet struck the ground, there was not so much as a sound. With years of practice, combined with skills that came with my vrykolakas nature, I was adept in the art of stealth.

Although intoxicated, his *mágos* senses did him credit. He spun to face me, his eyes widening in shock.

I straightened to full height and met his gaze.

"WHAT!? What do you want?" he squealed, his demeanor quickly shifting to one of terror.

"Oh… not much… just for you to die," I replied, my tone neutral and devoid of any inflection.

His eyes, already looking saucers, continued to widen, as he came to terms with his peril.

"*Shikari*!" he hissed, his face turning whiter than the robe he was wearing.

Immediately, he began a series of complicated hand movements, muttering under his breath as he did so. He was beginning a spell of immobilization and I would need to move quickly.

I leapt forward, utilizing the full extent of my vrykolakas speed. If there had been any witnesses, all they would have seen was a brief blur of motion. Reaching Hashem, I wrapped one arm around his shoulders and the other around his head. In a single decisive movement, I twisted it sideways and down to the right. There was an audible crack. He went limp in my arms—his neck broken.

Rather than letting the corpse drop to the ground, I dragged it to the top of the staircase. With a single arm supporting the lifeless torso, I pivoted and hurled the body with all my strength, pushing against its back as I did so. It landed headfirst about halfway down the flight of steps, then tumbled the remaining distance, limbs flailing grotesquely, before coming to rest in a crumpled heap at the bottom. The dull thud of its impact echoed through the stairwell, a stark reminder of the violence that had just transpired.

Surveying the scene, I allowed myself a satisfied smile. Anyone who discovered the body would likely assume he had fallen down the steps in a drunken stupor. The last thing this city needed was another suspicious, high-profile death—one that would alert the authorities and make my task more challenging. This way, his demise would be dismissed as a tragic accident, leaving me free to continue my mission undeterred.

As I stood at the top of the stairs, gazing at my handiwork, the silence was broken by the sound of footsteps and laughing voices. A group of men had just entered the alley.

Without hesitation, I bolted in the opposite direction, my muscles propelling me forward into a sprint. As I approached the end of the alley, I gradually slowed my pace, transitioning into a brisk walk. Emerging onto the main thoroughfare, I found myself engulfed by the bustling chaos of the city streets. Casting a quick glance over my shoulder to ensure I wasn't being pursued, I seamlessly merged into the crowd making their way toward the temple.

Chapter Nineteen

Kallian

480 BCE

Over the course of the past few months, little of note had transpired. Kallian was relieved that winter had come and gone. It had been brutally cold and the rain had been incessant.

It was now early spring, Kallian's favorite time of year. The game was plentiful, and the weather was relatively mild, especially compared to the scorching heat of summer. At its zenith, the sun could blister the earth, turning rocks into impromptu frying pans for eggs cracked open under its searing rays.

Although he had not shared an intimate connection with Aristion since their kiss, they had grown remarkably close. Aristion was a veritable treasure trove of knowledge, and they had whiled away many an evening discussing the pivotal events and conflicts that had shaped the rise of the Persian Empire. Despite appearing not much older than himself, Kallian was taken aback by the depth of understanding possessed by his friend and mentor. In many ways, Aristion reminded him of the venerable historian Gerasimos, who had taught classes at the *agōgē*. Gerasimos had peacefully passed away in his sleep at the age of seventy, a year before Kallian's departure.

He walked up to the city gates and smiled at the familiar faces of the guards. They wore embroidered tunics in vibrant hues of blue and gold, adorned with intricate patterns that symbolized their rank and allegiance. Over their tunics, they had reinforced leather cuirasses, offering both protection and flexibility. Their finely crafted helmets featured decorative crests and plumes that shimmered in the sunlight, and metal cheek guards framed their stern yet approachable faces.

Each guard carried a long spear with a shaft engraved with traditional motifs. Curved scimitars hung from their ornate belts, ready for swift action if needed. Their sandals, laced up to the calves, completed their ensemble, blending functionality with distinct elegance. Despite their formidable appearance, the guards' eyes held a warmth of familiarity, nodding as he approached them.

"Looks like your hunting expedition was a great success," one of them remarked, glancing at the bulging pack slung over his shoulder.

Kallian grinned.

"Very—three rabbits and a pheasant."

He stopped, opened his pack and proffered one of the rabbits to the closest guard.

"Here, take one home to Amaya—It will make for an excellent stew."

The guard smiled gleefully and took the rabbit without so much as a second thought.

"Thank you, she'll love it!"

"I'm happy to oblige—it's always a delight to put a smile on Amaya's face!" Kallian laughed.

The idle banter persisted until Kallian finally excused himself, bidding them farewell before making his way into the city. His stomach growled in protest, a clear indication of his hunger. He couldn't wait to return home and prepare the two remaining rabbits over a crackling fire.

After a short detour to a market stall to pick up some vegetables, Kallian rounded the corner onto the street where their shop was located. Despite the sun dipping behind the city's outer wall, the heat remained oppressive, showing no signs of relenting even as night approached. A visit to the baths with Aristion was definitely in order and needed to be added to the evening's agenda.

~

Kallian was already in the steaming water when Aristion arrived. He had gone on ahead, since his mentor had been obliged to make a make a couple of quick deliveries after dinner.

Although Kallian and Aristion had become very close as friends, Kallian had not succeeded in putting aside his deeper feelings for Aristion. As Aristion stripped off his clothes and stood naked before him, stretching his tired limbs, Kallian felt his heart quicken. He had fallen hard for the man, and despite his attempts to suppress his feelings, he had failed miserably.

The warmth of Aristion's skin, the ripple of his muscles as he moved, and the casual intimacy they shared made Kallian's desire burn brighter. Every glance and every touch, however innocent, sent waves of longing through him. It was torture and delight intertwined, a constant battle between his heart and his willpower.

Kallian couldn't help but steal glances at Aristion. The sight of him, relaxed and unaware of the turmoil he caused, made Kallian's resolve falter. He knew he had to keep his feelings hidden, to protect their friendship and avoid complicating their lives.

Aristion glanced in his direction, caught Kallian staring and grinned. Their eyes locked, the chemistry between them evident. However, as quickly as the moment had come, it passed. Aristion broke eye contact and walked to the edge of the pool, his semi aroused shaft swinging from side to side. Obviously, the feelings Kallian experienced for Aristion were mutual, although neither acted on them.

As Kallian stood in the waist-deep water at the bottom of the steps leading into the pool, he felt his own manhood respond to the sight of the man before him. It only took a few beats of his heart before it began to throb and rise vertically from the black mass of hair at his groin. Realizing that it was now visible above the waterline, Kallian took a deep breath and quickly submerged, allowing the water to envelop him.

Feeling a little abashed, he sighed inwardly. Honoring the agreement between them was going to be more challenging than anything he had ever faced at the *agōgē*.

His breath spent, Kallian surfaced and met Aristion's eyes. "That rabbit was excellent!" Aristion remarked.

He was now in the water and acting as if he had not noticed the state of Kallian's manhood, obviously attempting to break the sexual tension with some idle banter.

"Thanks, I may go hunting again tomorrow—unless you need me for something?"

"Sure, there's not much to do right now anyway."

Kallian smiled in response, then ducked his head back under the water. When he resurfaced, he swept his long black hair away from his face, causing it to cascade down his back.

For nearly a candlemark, the two men bathed in silence, though the same couldn't be said for the thoughts swirling through Kallian's mind. They were dominated by a fervent longing to be wrapped around Aristion—their lips locked and tongues entwined.

"I'm going to head back to the shop. Did you want to come, or are you going to soak a while longer?" Aristion queried.

"I'm done, let's go."

Throwing caution to the wind, Kallian exited the water without attempting to hide the desire he felt for his mentor. His shaft was still hard, extending up his abdomen to his belly button. Out of the corner of his eye, he observed Aristion's gaze linger on the evidence of their mutual attraction before quickly averting his eyes. Kallian couldn't help but smile. If Aristion did not want to engage with him intimately, he wasn't going to make it easy for him.

Kallian stood confidently, letting the water drip from his body, his long black hair clinging to his back and shoulders. The steam from the bath swirled around him, adding an almost ethereal quality to the moment. Aristion's brief, heated glance had revealed more than words ever could. The sexual tension between them was now crackling like an intense fire, and Kallian could see the struggle in Aristion's eyes as he fought to maintain his composure. Satisfied with the response he had elicited from Aristion, he began to dress.

~

After a quick drink at the inn that was adjacent to the baths, the two men slowly made their way home. It had been a long day and Kallian was exhausted.

Just as they rounded the corner onto their street, Aristion froze and took hold of Kallian's arm.

"You see that man in our doorway?" he said, motioning toward the shop with his head.

"Yes." Kallian replied, after a quick glance.

"Go see what he wants. I forgot something and need to run another errand before we turn in for the night."

"Sure—I'll see you soon!" Kallian responded with a smile and then turned, taking off down the street.

When he reached the shop, he was greeted by a man who appeared to be in his early fifties, clad in garments marking him as a member of the order of Zoroastrian Warrior Clerics. The man's robe bore three stripes, one of gold and two of blue, running vertically down the front and back, presumably indicating his rank. While Kallian had some knowledge of the order, there was much about its inner workings that remained unfamiliar to him.

"Hello, how can I help you?" Kallian inquired, as he opened the door.

The man looked directly into Kallian's eyes and paused before answering. There was something about him that was positively menacing, sending a shiver down the entire length of Kallian's spine. His gaze was intense and unwavering, and a dark aura seemed to cling to him, provoking a sense of foreboding.

"Who was that man you were with?" he demanded, his tone authoritarian and reflective of a person who gave, rather than took orders.

Even before the man spoke, Kallian had surmised that the stranger was dangerous and he would need to tread carefully.

"My employer," Kallian replied, deferentially.

"Why did he turn and leave?"

The heckles on the back of Kallian's head were now standing on end and a feeling of dread descended over him.

"He had to run a quick errand and will be back shortly."

"I see—no matter," the man responded curtly. He then took a moment to look Kallian up and down before proceeding. "I require a sword—the best you have. My father is arriving early tomorrow morning and I'd like to present him with a gift."

Kallian opened the door, smiling.

"That won't be a problem. In fact, I think I have exactly what you need. We acquired a beautiful weapon from a trader a few weeks ago."

With that, Kallian entered the building and the man followed, his eyes glancing from side to side, taking in the surroundings as he did so.

~

A few hours later Kallian glanced up from the ledger he was studying, as the bell above the door jingled. Aristion was standing in the entryway with a burlap sack of produce thrown casually over his shoulder.

"How did it go with the customer?" he inquired, dropping the bag to the ground next to the counter.

"Great—he purchased *Rashnu*!" Kallian replied, referring to the sword in their inventory that had been named after a Persian deity, the Zoroastian Angel of Justice. It was the most expensive weapon they had possessed and was worth nearly as much as all the others combined.

"That's wonderful news!" Aristion exclaimed, smiling broadly.

"Yes, but I'm relieved he's gone. There was something about the man that made the blood in my veins run cold. I hope he never comes back!"

"He's got what he wants—I wouldn't worry about it," Aristion responded with a shrug, before walking in the direction of the practice area. "Fancy some sword practice before we retire?"

Kallian beamed and grabbed his weapon.

Chapter Twenty

Aristion

480 BCE

A few days had passed since the sale of *Rashnu*. It had brought in a hefty amount of gold, which enabled me to drastically expand the shop's inventory with items that could be passed on for a quick profit. The new weapons would also encourage the residents of Sardis to keep coming back. This was essential, as many of them provided much-needed intelligence regarding the intent and disposition of the Persian forces.

Kallian had been gone for the day. In fact, over the last few months, he had spent more time hunting than working. It did not matter to me, since I only required his presence when I had to be elsewhere. In fact, it gave me pleasure to allow him the freedom to do something he enjoyed. He was always radiant when he returned—his eyes sparkling and cheeks flushed with excitement. Presenting me with the game he had snagged with his bow, he reminded me of a house cat dropping a mouse at its owner's feet. The scent of the forest clung to him, a mix of pine, oak, and cedar, characteristic of the lush vegetation around Sardis. The satisfaction in his voice was unmistakable as he recounted his day's adventures.

After cleaning and adding the last of the new weapons to my ledger, I leaned back against the support of my chair, stretched, and let out a long exhale. It was now early evening, and the time had dragged. It had been a slow day, with only a handful of customers. The shop felt eerily quiet and the fading light cast long shadows across the room, illuminating the rows of meticulously crafted weapons lining the walls.

Rather than waiting for Kallian to return, I wrote him a brief note, grabbed my sword and walked toward the front door. I had arranged to meet the Persian officer, Ghazi, for a few drinks. It had been a while since I had seen him and he was always a wealth of information.

Closing the door firmly behind me, I stepped out onto the street, greeted by the tranquil embrace of twilight. The sun had dipped below the outer walls, casting a soft, golden hue over the city. In this gentle glow, the harsh contrasts of daylight had dissolved, replaced by a serene ambiance that enveloped the streets in a comforting embrace.

I had only walked a few steps when my senses detected movement. Given the time, there were few people in the area where the shop was located. The businesses that lined the street had long closed their doors, and the street, usually filled with the hum of commerce, was devoid of activity. The distant sound of a lone cart rattling down a nearby street echoed faintly, underscoring the emptiness. I felt a subtle shift in the atmosphere, a hint of anticipation as if the quiet itself was holding its breath, waiting for something to break the stillness.

Glancing around, I couldn't locate the source of the disturbance, so I continued down the street toward the inn. The evening air was still, and the distant hum of the city had quieted. However, I had not gone more than a few steps when I heard the distinct scuff of a boot against the stone pavers behind me. The noise felt out of place, particularly since my initial scan had not revealed anyone nearby. Instinctively, I reached for the hilt of my sword and swiftly pivoted on my heel, my senses heightened.

Five men, swords drawn and dressed in the livery of the Zoroastrian Warrior Clerics, had completely blocked the street behind me. Their malicious grins were unsettling, and when I looked into the eyes of the man closest to me, I was met by a cold, fierce determination. His gaze was unwavering, like that of a predator sizing up its prey. The silence of the deserted street amplified the tension, the air heavy with the promise of imminent violence. Each of the men seemed poised, their stances indicating both confidence and readiness, as if they had been anticipating this encounter. The narrow street now felt claustrophobic, the walls of the surrounding buildings pressing in, leaving no room for escape.

Without a second thought, I unsheathed my weapon and prepared to close the distance to engage them. However, I hesitated when another four men emerged from the alley to their right, followed by the sound of footsteps in the direction I had been walking. Glancing over my shoulder, I discovered another ten clerics blocking the street ahead of me. I was trapped!

Opposed by nineteen clerics, I considered my options. It would be a tough fight, but they were no match for me, especially since there did not appear to be a *mágos* present in their party. No sooner than the thought crossed my mind, it felt wrong. No *mágos*? That couldn't be correct. Clerics without the support of a *mágos* would not be able to take me down—and they knew it! However, I did not have time to deliberate further, since all nineteen clerics let forth a roar, broke into a run, and began to close the distance quickly. Completely encircled and with no viable options left, I had to act fast to clear a path and put as much distance between myself and them as possible.

Rather than heading back in the direction of the shop, which would take me further away from the city gates, I charged at the ten clerics in front of me—sprinting at the full extent of my vrykolakas speed. To them, I probably seemed like a blur of motion, a human form moving so fast that their eyes would struggle to follow. It would be like trying to focus on an arrow that had been released from a bow.

I slammed into the first cleric with my right shoulder, the impact so forceful that his entire rib cage collapsed with an audible crack. The blow lifted him off his feet, sending him airborne, his body twisting in a grotesque arc before crashing to the ground twenty paces behind where he had been standing. Simultaneously, I pivoted and brought up my sword arm, the blade flashing in the dim light as I decapitated the man to his left. Blood sprayed in an arc as his head separated cleanly from his body. Without pausing, I completed the movement with a swift, precise slice across the throat of the cleric to his right, the sharp iron cutting through flesh and sinew with ease. His eyes widened in shock before he crumpled to the ground, clutching at his neck in a futile attempt to staunch the flow.

The seven who were still standing did not hesitate, even in the face of my ferocious attack. They had been well trained and knew that any form of reticence on their part would probably result in their death. *Shamshirs* arced towards me from all sides, appearing to move sluggishly, as if time itself had slowed to a fraction of its normal pace. The reality of the situation was that it was simply an illusion, one created by the sheer magnitude of the speed at which I was moving—relative to theirs. With a slight move of my face to the right, a blade passed through the air where my head had been, and then with a twist to the left, another passed across the front of my torso, slicing the fabric of my clothing at waist level.

My mind was now a void, emptied of all but the present moment. I existed in a trance-like state, where every thought and sensation was consumed by a graceful, well-practiced flow of movement. It was as if I had surrendered myself entirely to *The Dance of the Vrykolakas*, a primal rhythm that pulsed through my veins, guiding every step, every strike. My body moved with lethal precision, each motion seamless and fluid.

A swift sidestep took me out of the path of another blade, my own sword flashing in retaliation, cleaving through muscle and bone. Blood sprayed in a fine mist, but I was already moving on to the next target. My senses were acute; I could hear the rapid, panicked breaths of my opponents and see the fear flickering in their eyes, despite their resolve.

Another cleric lunged at me, his *shamshir* aimed at my heart. I parried with a deft flick of my wrist and followed up with a swift kick to his midsection, sending him staggering back, off-balance and vulnerable. In one fluid motion, I spun and slashed, my blade effortlessly slicing through his abdomen.

As the fight raged on, my movements became a seamless blur of precision and power. My sword arced overhead, and with a decisive leap forward, I brought it directly down. The blade met its mark, severing a hand that still clutched its *shamshir*. The dismembered hand tumbled to the street, joining the severed heads that continued to roll beneath the feet of the combatants.

Leaning to the right, I avoided another blade that passed harmlessly over my head. Without the slightest hesitation, I lashed back with my left foot, winding its wielder. The cleric doubled over, gasping for breath. No sooner had I made contact than I began a graceful spin that ended in a low crouch. With my sword poised, I struck upward, the blade piercing directly into the soft palate beneath his jaw

With the entire force of my vrykolakas strength at my disposal, I then catapulted myself up from my crouch, over the heads of the three remaining clerics. I completed the movement with a back spin and came to rest behind them. One was still incapacitated from the kick to his stomach, but the other two began a turn to face me. However, with one quick thrust and a final swing of my sword, they never completed it. As they fell dead to the ground, I briefly met the eyes of the remaining cleric.

Hunched over and clutching his stomach, he was glaring at me with unbridled hatred.

The entire fight had taken place in just a few heartbeats. However, the nine remaining clerics who had been in the vicinity of my shop were now sprinting towards me and had managed to close half the distance. I had no doubt I could handle them, but there was still the distinct possibility that a *mágos* was present.

Erring on the side of caution, I turned and was about to make a run for the city gates, only to find my path blocked by at least another ten clerics—and in their midst, I could make out the distinctive robes and colors of a *mágos*.

Well—shit!

Given their numbers, they had not left anything to chance. They had brought the entire garrison to apprehend me, including its last *mágos*—the other having left Sardis a couple of weeks earlier with an entourage of twenty clerics. From what I had gleaned from my contacts at the time, there had been reports of vrykolakas activity close to the coast, and he had been sent to investigate.

Out of options, I pivoted with the intent to break through the group of clerics that were almost upon me. Although the route would take me deeper into the city, I had no choice. However, it was the last move I made, as I began to feel the incapacitating magic being dispensed by the *mágos* take root. The foul taint of his machinations began to course through my blood, and I could feel my limbs becoming sluggish, no longer responding to my mental commands. Inwardly, I let out a groan of frustration and resigned myself to my fate. The *mágos* now had me completely under his power, one that held me in a vice-like grip—completely immobilizing me.

The clerics advanced with grim satisfaction, their swords glinting in the dim light. I could see the cold determination in their eyes, and I knew they had no intention of showing mercy. The *mágos*, standing at the center of the formation, watched with an expression of calm control, his hands still weaving the spell that bound me.

My mind raced, searching for any possible escape, but the magic was too strong. My muscles refused to cooperate, and I could feel the strength draining from my body. The clerics surrounded me, their formation tightening like a noose. I had fought to the best of my ability, but the odds had finally caught up with me. The *mágos*' power was absolute, and I was now at his mercy.

Chapter Twenty-One

Kallian

480 BCE

Kallian was tired. He had been hunting game for the best part of the day and the fruits of his labor, two large rabbits, were slung over his right shoulder. However, even with his stomach growling in protest, the only thought on his mind was a long soak at the baths.

Making his way up the final incline of the road that through the northern gates of the city, he paused to take in the beauty of the sun that was about to disappear behind the mountains to the west. The view from this vantage point never ceased to amaze him—especially at this time of day.

He was about to continue his ascent, when he heard the sound of a large number of men on horseback coming through the city gates. Turning, he quickly realized that he was directly in their path and would be run down if he did not move quickly.

Stepping off the road, he took in the composition of the unit as they passed him. It was none other than the Satrap himself and fifty of his personal guard. The Satrap, clad in traditional Persian attire, rode at the front. He wore a richly embroidered robe of deep purple, signifying his high status, and a tall, cylindrical hat known as a *tiara*, adorned with gold and precious stones. His stern face, marked by years of leadership, was partially concealed by a meticulously groomed beard.

The personal guard followed closely behind, each warrior a paragon of strength and discipline. They rode on well-bred horses, their presence formidable. Each guard wore a *thorakion*, a leather cuirass reinforced with metal scales, which provided both flexibility and protection. Over their colorful tunics, each bearing the emblem of the Satrap, they had quivers filled with arrows strapped to their backs, and bows hanging from their saddles

Where were they going with such urgency? It was rare for the Satrap to leave the city and he would not be doing so without good cause.

As his eyes followed their descent, Kallian's attention was drawn to the grasslands on the northern side of the river Hermos.

He froze.

An army engulfed the entire valley and thousands of soldiers were scurrying around like busy bees. From what he could ascertain from his vantage point, they were in the process of erecting tents and were doing so in haste, probably in an attempt to complete their task before nightfall.

Ominous as it was, it was the pavilion-like structure at the army's center that caused Kallian's emotional state to shift from curiosity and concern to dread. As he took in the banner on the tent's pinnacle, his heart skipped a beat, and it felt as if a swarm of insects had erupted from his chest, deluging his body and prickling his skin.

Xerxes! The fourth King of Kings of the Achaemenid Empire was in Sardis.

Given Kallian's intimate knowledge of the region's politics, the presence of Xerses and an army of this magnitude could only mean one thing. It had been long rumored that Xerses desired revenge for the failure of Darius I, his father, marked by his defeat at the Battle of Marathon. Obviously, the time had finally arrived. The fourth King of Kings of the Achaemenid Empire was preparing to invade Greece.

After taking a few deep breaths to calm himself, Kallian began the essential task of estimating the enemies troop composition and number. Once done, he turned and walked briskly towards the city gates. He had to inform Aristion.

It did not take long before the corner of the street where their shop was situated came into view. As he approached, he noticed a heightened level of activity, unusual for this time of day. A crowd had gathered near the corner, their attention fixed on something. Whatever it was, he would have to get closer to discern its source.

Kallian's curiosity began to get the better of him, and he picked up his pace. It was not long before he came up behind an elderly man who was looking down the street in the direction of their shop. This fact alone was a cause for concern, and he began to feel a tightening in his chest.

Standing on his toes and craning his head to look over the man's shoulder, the subject matter of what was capturing the crowd's attention, came into view. Kallian froze and his blood ran cold.

Aristion stood in the center of the street, approximately fifteen cart lengths away from Kallian's position. Around him, a throng of at least twenty Zoroastrian Warrior Clerics formed a formidable circle. His attention seemed transfixed on a figure standing a few paces in front of him, a man clad in a striking blue and gold striped robe. This was the same cleric who had visited their shop a few days prior to purchase Rashnu.

So many thoughts raced through Kallian's mind that he could scarcely think straight. Why had they apprehended Aristion? What could he do to aid his mentor? Why was he frozen in place? Aristion still wielded his sword and undoubtedly possessed the skill to break through the encircling men. Run, damn it—RUN!

Well, if Aristion wasn't going to act, Kallian would. With dusk approaching, it offered a degree of cover. A narrow side street ran behind the row of houses to the right of the clerics. He casually turned and retraced his steps down the street, then veered left into the alley, careful not to draw any undue attention. If the clerics were aware of Aristion, there was a strong chance he would also come under suspicion.

Unceremoniously dropping the rabbits, he walked past a number of buildings, until he reached a point at which he was level with the clerics who were on the other side. Bow slung over his back, he began to climb. There were many rough foot and hand holds in the uneven stone work of the structure he had picked for his assent. Unlike many of the wooden buildings that surrounded it, this one was made of stone and had a flat roof. Kallian was intimately familiar with all of the businesses close to the shop and this one was a forge, belonging to a rotund jovial man called Fahid.

Kallian made short work of the climb and within a few seconds had reached the top. He crawled to the far edge of the building and peered down at the scene unfolding below. Several clerics now held lit torches, and in the eerie light they cast, he could clearly make out the features of the man in the blue and gold striped robe. A large number of bodies were scattered around him, all garbed in the attire of Zoroastrian Warrior Clerics. Aristion had obviously put up a fight and had wreaked havoc on their number, which left Kallian a little perplexed. Given the number of clerics he had killed, why had Aristion stopped fighting and chosen to surrender instead? He did not look wounded and was not being restrained. He was simply standing there.

From his vantage point, Kallian's attention fell on the ugly bald man in the striped robe. The man's round, greasy face reflected the torchlight as he appeared to be speaking to Aristion. Although Kallian could not hear what was being said, he could see the man's mouth twisting into a sneer, droplets of spittle flying with each word. This did not bode well!

The man gestured to a couple of the clerics who, without hesitation, walked over to Aristion and disarmed him, casting his sword to the ground. Task done, they stepped back quickly, as if Aristion were a deadly snake, holding their *shamshirs* in a guard position, ready to ward off any sudden attack.

The bald man withdrew his own sword and began to walk slowly towards Aristion. His movements were deliberate and menacing, each step exuding a sense of cold, calculated malice. Kallian's blood ran cold as he watched, understanding that this man had no intention of taking Aristion captive. The torchlight flickered ominously, casting long shadows that seemed to mirror the man's dark intent. The air was thick with tension, and Kallian could feel his heart pounding in his chest, the realization of imminent danger settling over him like a shroud.

NO! This couldn't be happening! The sheer intensity of the emotions flooding through Kallian—fear mingled with burning rage—propelled him to his feet. In that moment, he didn't care about the overwhelming odds or the possibility of his own demise. He refused to stand by while someone he loved was threatened. The mere thought of losing Aristion was unbearable, a visceral pain akin to having his heart torn from his chest.

Kallian unslung his bow, simultaneously pulling an arrow from his quiver. Without a second thought, he notched the arrow and pulled the string of the bow back to his cheek. He was well versed at taking down fast moving game and the fat bald man would offer little challenge. He released the arrow and let out a breath as it flew towards it target.

The fat, bald warrior cleric who had just reached Aristion was in the process of raising his *shamshir* to strike him down when the arrow took him directly in the heart. The look of unbridled glee that had been on his face was replaced by one of shock, which quickly turned to horror as he staggered back, staring at the shaft protruding from his chest. He was likely dead before his mind could fully grasp what had occurred—perhaps even before his body hit the ground with a dull thud.

What followed next was surreal and incomprehensible to Kallian. The crowd that had gathered to witness the spectacle, along with the clerics encircling Aristion, froze in place as if held by invisible bonds. A heavy silence descended upon the street below, punctuated only by the soft rustle of clothing and the occasional murmur of subdued voices.

Then, in a moment that seemed to defy the tension of the scene, Kallian watched as the corners of Aristion's mouth curl up into a menacing smile. Pivoting, he turned to face the two clerics who had disarmed him. Though Kallian had not been able to hear the exact words uttered by the cleric he had just killed, he had no trouble discerning what Aristion said to the men before him.

"DON'T MOVE!"

Aristion then stooped and calmly picked up his sword. However, the clerics did not appear to react. They simply stood there, barely flinching at the threat Aristion now posed. It made no sense. The only conclusion Kallian could draw was that they were probably in a state of shock after witnessing their commander take an arrow to the chest.

Finally, as if they were attempting to break free of some invisible bonds, the two clerics appeared to snap out of their stupor and began to stagger forward, swords raised, their movements unusually clumsy for well-trained warriors. Before they had taken two steps, Aristion swung his weapon in a single long arc and decapitated their heads.

Kallian, although surprised by the turn of events, was not one to miss an opportunity. He quickly notched another arrow and set his sights on another cleric. At the same time, the other warriors, who had apparently recovered from the shock of what had just happened, burst into motion.

By the time the arrow found its intended target, Aristion was weaving through the mass of warriors in a graceful, deadly dance. His movements were almost inhumanly swift, his sword slicing through them as easily as a knife through soft butter.

Kallian couldn't believe his eyes. Aristion seemed to be moving faster and faster, his speed and agility far beyond that of any man Kallian had ever seen. Each swing of his sword was precise and lethal, every step calculated to perfection. The clerics, despite their training and numbers, were no match for the whirlwind of iron and flesh that Aristion had become.

The scene was mesmerizing and terrifying all at once. Aristion's face was a mask of fierce concentration, his eyes blazing with an otherworldly intensity. His sword glinted in the torchlight, a blur of silver as it struck down one opponent after another. The warriors around him fell in quick succession, unable to counter his relentless onslaught.

The fight was over, almost as quicky as it had begun. The crowd of terrified spectators were in the process of scattering and Aristion was now standing motionless in the center of the street, directly below where Kallian was perched. He was surrounded by a sea of bodies. Every single warrior cleric, bar one, was dead. The sole survivor was crawling away from the scene, leaving a trail of blood on the stone beneath him.

Aristion turned and looked up at Kallian. He smiled and raised the pommel of his sword to his forehead in a salute. With his free hand, he made a quick gesture, signaling Kallian to head to their prearranged rendezvous point. Then, after a swift glance to survey the street to his left and right, he sprinted away toward the gate on the far side of the city. Kallian surmised that Aristion's intention was likely to exit Sardis before any news of the confrontation could spread.

Taking a few final seconds to survey the carnage below, Kallian inhaled deeply. He then slung the bow over his shoulder, walked to the far side of the roof, and dropped out of sight, just as the sun disappeared behind the mountain range west of the city.

Chapter Twenty-Two

Aristion

480 BCE

As I rounded the corner onto the street that intersected with the one where our shop was located, I spotted a horse tethered to a post beside the local apothecary. I had visited the establishment several times over the previous winter to purchase medicinals for Kallian, who had fallen ill from eating tainted meat.

The owner of the horse was nowhere to be seen, so I decided to take it. Riding would allow me to make better time and attract less attention. The inhabitants of Sardis would find it odd to see a man sprinting through the streets at dusk. However, on horseback, I would simply be mistaken for a messenger, a common sight often seen traversing the city's streets.

As I rode at a heavy trot, restraining my desire to push the horse into a gallop, I thought back to my encounter with the *mágos*.

~

With a pinched face, frigid features, and mouth twisted into a snarl, the *mágos* literally spat the word.

"*Galla*!"

Unable to move my limbs and groaning from the strain, I briefly closed my eyes in an attempt to gather my strength. I desperately needed to free myself from his hold.

"I could smell your taint when I came into your shop. You are a vile, disgusting, and soulless creature. It will be a pleasure to send you back to *Duzakh*!"

Duzakh was the Persian word for Hades. From my understanding of Zoroastrianism, it was seen as a deep well—terrifying because it was dark, stinking, and extremely narrow. In *Duzakh*, the smallest of the creatures, the *xrafstars*, were thought to be as big as mountains, and their sole purpose was to devour and destroy the souls of the damned.

As he spoke, I continued to wrestle with the magical bonds that were restraining me. Relentlessly, I pushed with the entire strength of my will—but each time I did so, the barbs of the taint in my blood grew stronger. The magic was foul, and it held me rooted to the spot. No matter how hard I tried, I remained immobilized. It was pointless. I was completely under his control and at his mercy; something he was not predisposed to offer me.

As the reality of my situation finally took hold, I thought of Kallian. With that, something finally snapped. I experienced an intense pain in my heart, as if it had been pierced by a blade. The realization that I would never see him again literally tore me apart.

The *mágos*, finally tiring from his verbal tirade, began to move towards me. The maliciousness emanating from him as I looked into his eyes left no doubt. He meant to kill me—right here and now. There was no mistaking his demeanor and the message it conveyed. Its meaning would have been crystal clear to even the most obtuse minds among humanity.

Finally reaching me, he raised his *shamshir*. I braced myself, knowing that my death was imminent. Out of options, I pushed against his hold one final time, only to be met with an impenetrable wall of magic. I let out a final breath and resigned myself to my fate, the strike that would end my life.

Just as the arc of his sword reached its epitaph and was about to begin its final descent, the *mágos* let out a gasp. His eyes widened in shock, and he reflexively released his grip on the weapon. The *shamshir* clattered to the ground. An arrow protruded from his chest, and blood rapidly spread in ever-increasing circles across his garments, staining the fabric a deep crimson.

The *mágos* staggered back, and within a few heartbeats, the light drained from the man's eyes. It was as if a fire had been extinguished by a sudden deluge of water.

As the *mágos*' corpse crumpled to the ground, I couldn't help but notice his face, frozen in a visage of disbelief and horror. His eyes were wide open, staring blankly into the void, while his mouth hung agape in a silent scream. The features were etched with the shock of sudden realization, as if the truth of his impending death had struck him in those final moments. His once arrogant expression was now replaced with an eternal mask of fear and astonishment.

Kallian!

Immediately, my control returned. It flooded back into me like a torrent. With the death of the *mágos*, the magical bonds that held me had simply vanished.

In exaltation, I smiled and turned towards the two clerics who had disarmed me. My gaze locked onto theirs. "DON'T MOVE!" I commanded, my voice laden with compulsion. The clerics froze, their expressions going blank under my influence. I bent down and retrieved my sword from where it had been cast aside.

The rest was inevitable, just like the path of the sun across the heavens. Although I knew that Kallian would witness it, I had no choice. I tapped into the full skill and speed of my true nature—that of a vrykolakas.

~

It did not take long to reach the gates on the far side of Sardis. To my relief, the guards were relaxed, their postures slouched and their expressions bored, indicating they had no knowledge of what had transpired. I gave them a brief wave of greeting, my heart pounding in my chest. They looked disinterested, merely replying with curt nods before returning to their idle chatter.

The sprawling countryside stretched out before me, a vast expanse of rolling hills and lush fields. The sounds of the city—clattering carts, shouting vendors, and the murmur of countless voices—faded into the background, replaced by the gentle rustling of leaves and the occasional call of a distant bird. As I absorbed the serene landscape, my muscles began to relax, and my mind started to clear. The vastness of the countryside offered a profound sense of peace and a much-needed chance to gather my thoughts.

Chapter Twenty-Three

Kallian

480 BCE

After a quick descent from the roof, Kallian dropped to the ground and made his way to the main street that led to the main gates of the city. As they came into view, he could see that they were shut and barred. Standing before them were four guards, different from the ones who had been stationed there when he had entered the city earlier. The shift must have changed with the setting sun. This worked in his favor, since they would not have any knowledge that he had just come back from his hunting excursion.

He casually strolled towards them and was relieved to see that one of them was the jovial man married to Amaya.

"*Salam*," he said with a smile, reaching out and grasping the others hand with a firm shake. "What's going on Armeen? I heard that there was a disturbance in the city."

"I have no idea Bijan. I've not been on duty long and a runner told us to shut the gates and keep them barred until we receive further orders," he responded with a shrug. There was a slight trace of concern in his eyes and his features creased into a grimace as he spoke.

"Damn! I was hoping get in a little night hunting! I'm in the mood for some rabbit and the market stalls are closed," Kallian said, feigning exasperation. "Any chance you can let me out? I'll get one for you too. I'm sure Amaya would appreciate it!"

"I'm sorry Bijan, but I'd be thrown in the cities deepest dungeon and left there to rot if I so much as touch the bar."

For a brief moment, Kallian considered resorting to force. It would be easy for him to take them. However, he genuinely liked Armeen and the thought of causing him harm did not appeal to him. The man had always treated Kallian well and they had even been out drinking a few times. The evenings with him had always been enjoyable and filled with mirth, since the man had a wicked sense of humor.

Kallian sighed and clapped the man on the back. "No worries, you old goat, I'm sure I'll be able to survive the night without a rabbit to fill my belly," he laughed.

"Get out of here kid and leave the old goat alone. Tonight is going to be a long one!" Armeen smiled, gesturing with his hand in a shooing motion, back down the street Kallian had just come along.

As he walked, Kallian began to deliberate. There were not many options left open to him and he needed to exit the city quickly. It would only be a matter of time before the news of Aristion's involvement in the killing of the clerics became public knowledge and by association, he would also be held to account.

Kallian's mind raced like a wild stallion, darting between possible options. Every obvious route seemed barred, like a fortress gate under siege. Short of hurling himself from the city walls to certain death below, he struggled to envision any means of escaping the iron grip of the city's boundaries.

As he approached the intersection close to the shop, he could not help but notice the sheer number of soldiers in the city streets. They were everywhere. From what he could tell, they were questioning the cities inhabitants and even knocking on doors. Kallian let out a groan. The net they were casting was closing in and there was little time left to act.

Rather than proceeding along his current route, he took a turn to his left and almost ran into a horse. About fifty men, all garbed in the clothing of an elite Persian cavalry unit, filled the area. The emblem on their tunics signified that this group was assigned to the city's defense. Some sat astride their horses, while others stood beside them, apparently waiting for orders. Their commanding officer, a lithe, bearded man in his early fifties, was conversing with a warrior cleric. As Kallian passed by, he caught snippets of their dialogue, hinting that the unit was preparing to leave the city in pursuit of a fugitive.

Aristion had escaped!

Kallian let out an exhale and with the release of breath, he felt an overwhelming sense of relief. Due to his own predicament, he had not really had the time to ponder on the subject of Aristion's fate, although it had always been in the back of his mind. Now, after hearing the news, he felt as if a great burden had been lifted from his shoulders.

As Kallian passed the last member of the troop, a warrior around his own age and build, the man lashed the reigns of his horse to a post and moved towards an alley, adjacent to where he had been standing. The warrior was tugging on his clothing as he walked and it was obvious to Kallian that he intended to relieve himself before the unit departed.

Kallian smiled. An opportunity had just availed itself. One that would allow him to escape from the confines of the city.

Rather than proceeding along the road, Kallian casually turned into the alley, following the young warrior. The man had his back to him and Kallian could hear him sighing with relief as he emptied his bladder. It was a blissful sigh, one that generally emanated from a man who had been dying to relieve himself for quite a while, a feeling Kallian knew all too well!

While it would have been all too easy to approach from behind and use his hunting knife to slit the man's throat, Kallian couldn't bring himself to do it. The thought of killing someone in such a manner, in cold blood, unsettled him. It lacked honor. He recalled an evening when Aristion had challenged him on this very point over a jug of ale.

"Kallian, we are at war. These people are your enemy. A situation may arise in which you have to carry out an action outside of your code of honor—even stab someone from behind. I assure you, if anyone in this city discovers your identity, they would not think twice about dismembering you!"

The conversation had gone on for a while and finally ended with Aristion stalking out of the room, shaking his head in exasperation.

"I swear, this honor of yours will be the death of you one day," was his final retort, as the door slammed behind him.

Walking silently, Kallian approached the warrior, who was finishing his business and giving the muscle between his legs a few brief shakes. Without hesitation or deliberation, Kallian struck, encircling the man's neck with his right arm, locking him in a chokehold. Simultaneously, he covered the man's mouth with his left hand to stifle any screams for help. Despite the warrior's struggles, Kallian's strength prevailed, preventing him from breaking free. Dragging the man back into a recess between two houses, Kallian intentionally fell backward, bringing the warrior down with him with an audible thud that nearly winded Kallian. However, he maintained his grip, his legs entwined around the warrior, immobilizing him completely. The struggle ended swiftly as the man slipped into unconsciousness.

Kallian removed the warrior's garments and then took some twine from his pack, which he carried for making snares to catch game. He bound the man's hands behind his back and repeated the procedure with his feet. Kallian then joined the two bindings together with another length of twine, ensuring the warrior could not straighten his legs to stand. Finally, once the man was secure, Kallian tore a strip from his own clothing and gagged him.

He was running out of time. The officer he had seen conversing with the cleric was now barking out orders, his voice sharp and commanding. The cavalry unit was preparing to depart, and the sounds of men mounting their horses and the clinking of armor filled the air.

Kallian donned the warrior's clothing and hastily placed the man's helmet on his head. The helmet, made of bronze with a rounded top, featured intricate etchings and a sturdy nose guard. After stooping to pick up the man's *shamshir*, which he attached to his newly acquired belt, he unceremoniously threw his bow, quiver, pack, and clothes over the unconscious man—completely covering the body. Given the limited time at his disposal, it was the best he could do. Hopefully, the man would not regain consciousness before Kallian had made his escape from the city.

With his disguise complete, Kallian sauntered toward the exit of the alley, internally lamenting the loss of his bow, a cherished gift from Aristion. However, he took solace in the fact that the warrior would likely have a bow of his own, strapped to the saddle of his horse. While it might not offer the same range as the bow he had given up, it would suffice for his needs.

As the calvary troop came into view, Kallian smiled. His timing was perfect. Almost everyone was mounted and some were even making their way down the road, led by their commander.

He looked down as he walked, carefully avoiding eye contact with any of the men. As the last of them nudged his horse into motion, Kallian swiftly leapt into his saddle with the practiced ease symbolic of a Persian cavalryman. With a quick shake of his reins, his horse sprang forward, and he seamlessly took his place at the rear of the unit.

Kallian let out an exhale of relief. Although he was still not free of city, the hardest aspect of his plan, the part that carried the most risk, was now complete.

It was not long before the towers flanking the city gates came into view. He could make out the features of his friend Armeen, standing stoically beside the right gate, casually watching the warriors pass by. Kallian forced himself to look away from his friend and drinking companion, avoiding any possibility of recognition as he made his final exit from the city. What surprised him was the degree of sadness and loss he felt over leaving Sardis. Although it was enemy territory, the city had been his home, and he had thoroughly enjoyed his life there over the past two years—especially the life he shared with Aristion.

Chapter Twenty-Four

Aristion

480 BCE

Once outside the city, I headed directly north into the valley, following the course of the river Hermos as it meandered its way to the area of the *Darya-ye Mazandaran* the Greeks called the *Egéo Pélagos*—the Aegean Sea.

Although it was now pitch-black, I could see perfectly. It was one of the many advantages my kind held over the common man. Since being reborn as a vrykolakas, I no longer experienced any deterioration of vision with the coming of night. In fact, my senses became even more heightened and acute. The night was my friend and it was something I often used to my advantage.

Reaching the river, I became aware of a multitude of campfires in valley to the north of the river, but with little time to consider their implication, I turned west along the road that led to the port city of Smyrna. However, my first stop would be the rendezvous point I had prearranged with Kallian. We had established it a few months after our arrival in Sardis as a precaution against the possibility of becoming separated if we were discovered—exactly the situation we now faced.

Although I had not seen any other riders, it would only be a matter of time before patrols were sent out at the behest of Mahan Abedzadeh, the commander of the Zoroastrian Warrior Clerics in Sardis. Even though he was not a *mágos*, his power was absolute. In the Persian military, the head of a Zoroastrian Warrior Cleric garrison—the *Khāné Atash Aršti*, outranked everyone, except for Darius, the King of the Achaemenid dynasty of Persia and the commander of the *Anusiya*. The *Anusiya*, or *Immortals*, were an elite heavy infantry unit comprised of 10,000 soldiers. They served as Darius' Imperial Guard, in addition to contributing to the ranks of the Persian Empire's standing army.

I picked up my pace and the horse was now moving at a gentle gallop. I did not want the beast to tire, so I avoided pushing the animal to its limits. It would take almost the entire night to reach the rendezvous point, a small cave on the north face of the mountain range, directly south of a fork in the valley. From this point, contingent on Kallian having made a successful escape, the two of us would continue on to Smyrna.

The journey was uneventful, likely because I had outpaced any patrols dispatched to find me, or perhaps Mahan Abedzadeh had simply assumed I was still hiding within the city walls. Yet, I swiftly dismissed the latter possibility; Mahan was exceptionally astute and would never leave a stone unturned. Hunting vrykolakas was a challenging task, even for the most talented of men. Someone like Mahan Abedzadeh would not have achieved his position if he had displayed a predisposition for careless.

Over the course of my journey, the only other travelers I encountered were members of a caravan, settled in for the night off to the side of the road. Fortunately, I spotted their tents from a distance, long before I drew near enough for the caravan guards to notice me.

Reaching the split in the valley, I left the road that had been running along the banks of the Hermos and headed directly south. I was now at the edge of the foothills of mountain range where the cave was located.

Rather than going directly to the cave, I rode over a small rise, dismounted and tied the reins of my horse to the stump of old tree. Laying prone to avoid discovery, I took up position on a small rock outcropping. It was a perfect vantage point, since it gave me a good view of the valley below. In the distance I could even make out the river that was disappearing behind the edge of the mountain range that denoted the valley divide.

Kallian would have to pass me to get to the cave, making this as good a place as any to await his arrival. From here, I could keep watch over the road below and prevent the possibility of being taken by surprise. The last thing I wanted was to end up trapped in a cave with an army of angry Persians wielding *shamshirs* outside.

Finally, I had time to relax, collect my thoughts and begin to process the events that had transpired. At the forefront of my mind was Kallian. Above all else, I was prayed to the God's that he had managed to get way. The thought that he may have been captured was not something I wanted to contemplate. They would be brutal and show no mercy in their attempt to get information out of him.

As I pondered the grim scenario of Kallian's potential capture, my thoughts turned increasingly bleak—dark, even. The more I dwelled on it, the more an uncomfortable sensation began to churn within me. It felt as if my blood was beginning to boil. I was consumed by rage, something I hadn't experienced for decades. It was the type of intense anger and loss of emotional control that all vrykolaka worked unceasingly to master and restrain. If Kallian was in their clutches, I would ride back to Sardis and tear down the walls of the *Khāné Atash Aršti* with my bare hands. I would free him or die in the attempt—for without him, my life would be over. I was in love with him. I never imagined I'd feel this way about another human being again, but somehow, that frustrating man, barely out of his youth, had carved his way into my heart. The rage I was experiencing was a testament to it!

I took a few deep breaths and quieted my mind—employing the techniques of my early vrykolaka training, until the rage I had been feeling subsided. Sighing, I closed my eyes and whispered another prayer to the God's.

Chapter Twenty-Five

Kallian

480 BCE

Kallian had been riding for most of the night. Without the benefit of the moon to light his way, he could barely make out the road, let alone the features of the other riders. This had worked in his favor, since it made the likelihood of being recognized as an imposter minimal.

He opted to stay with the troop as they veered westward, following the course of the Hermos. They were heading in the direction of the rendezvous point with Aristion, and the presence of his unwitting companions offered him a measure of protection. If a patrol had caught him riding alone, he may have been detained, especially due to what had transpired in the city.

Early in their journey, they had passed his favorite hunting grounds, close to where the Pactolus snaked its way down the foothills of Tmolos, the large mountain south of the city and merged with the Hermos. It was also the location of his altercation with the nobles. Although the fight had not been a pleasant experience, he would definitely miss basking in the sun and diving into the cool waters of the Pactolus—along with his hunting excursions close to its banks. It elicited a feeling best described as surreal. The landscape remained familiar and unchanged, yet his entire reality had shifted in what felt like the blink of an eye. His visit to that very area just a few short hours ago now seemed like a distant memory.

As he pondered the turn of events, the two riders directly in front of him began to talk, laughing as they did so.

"That army was a sight for sore eyes. I'd almost given up on Xerxes responding to what the Greeks had achieved at Marathon."

"Agreed! I lost two older brothers and three cousins at that battle!"

"I'm sorry to hear that."

"It's ok, I was young at the time and barely remember them."

"Well, the time of Greece is at an end. Xerxes will see to that!"

Kallian scoffed under his breath. Greece had not even been the aggressor. They had simply been defending themselves. If Darius had not invaded, the man's brothers would still be alive. Additionally, the over confidence of these men regarding Xerxes was misplaced. Greece was a formidable enemy and quite capable of defending itself.

Disgusted with the conversation, Kallian drew back on his reigns and opened up some distance. His back was aching and it was being exasperated by the annoyance he felt towards the men.

Since his arrival in Sardis, Kallian had barely ridden a horse. In fact, the last time had been during their reconnaissance—the one that had resulted in the discovery of the cave. That was almost two years ago.

Groaning, he reached back with his free hand and began to massage the lower area of his spine. As he did so, he recalled the events surrounding the fight in the city.

Kallian had been sure that Aristion was going to die, a thought that sickened him. Hopelessly outnumbered, there had been little hope that his assistance would be enough to tip the balance in his favor. Kallian's choice to kill the warrior cleric threatening Aristion had simply been an act of desperation, one that would afford Aristion a chance of escape, albeit small.

What had happened next, still perplexed Kallian. With the death of the cleric, Aristion had burst into motion. The speed at which he moved had seemed inhuman, almost surreal. Over the span of his relatively short life and training at the agōgē, Kallian had never witnessed anything like it. The astonishing feat of Aristion dispatching almost twenty clerics in a matter of mere heartbeats had left him in a state of utter disbelief and awe.

Kallian was still attempting to process the memory when the troop reached the fork in the valley. It would not be long before he would need to depart from the unit. They came to a halt and the officer in charge gave an order for the group of riders to divide. Fortunately for him, the rear section of the unit was told to take the road to the left, the one that led to Smyrna.

As his half of the troop commenced the next leg of its journey, Kallian gradually began to slow, letting the other riders gradually pull ahead. It was not long before the man directly in front of him completely disappeared from sight.

Coming to a stop, he listened, praying that his disappearance would go unnoticed. It did not take long before the sound of their horses subsided from his senses, replaced with the stoic silence of night. The only sound that could be heard was the slightly labored breathing of his horse, which let out a brief snort and scuffed the ground with one of its hooves. It was as if the beast was a little perturbed by the fact that they had been left behind.

Kallian finally let out a sigh of relief. He had not even been aware that he had been holding his breath. Gently shaking the reins and nudging the left side of the horse with his knee, the horse left the road and began to make its way into the foothills below the cave.

"Hey little brother, you took your time!" came a voice from above.

Aristion!

Kallian dismounted, just as a dark shadow dropped down beside his horse, startling the animal and causing it to jump back. Kallian, still with one foot in a stirrup, fell to the ground, landing on his buttocks.

Aristion let out laugh, "I see you riding skills still have room for improvement!"

"Dammit Aristion, that was totally your fault—frightening my horse like that!"

"How's the saying go, only a poor craftsman blames his tools," Aristion replied, still chuckling.

"True, except for the fact that I'm not blaming the damn horse, I'm blaming you!"

Kallian felt a hand grasp his wrist. Within the space of a heartbeat, he had been unceremoniously pulled to his feet, which brought him face to face with his mentor, companion and friend. He was so close, that he could feel Aristion's breath on his cheek. The grip released and an arm encircle his waist, pulling him into a tight embrace.

"I was worried about you little one!"

As he spoke, Aristion reached out with a hand and gently caressed the side of his face, sweeping long black strands away from his eyes. Kallian's hair was in complete disarray, since he lost his *sarband* when falling from his horse.

Aristion drew even closer, their lips almost touching. As their gaze met, Kallian's vision became transfixed and he lost himself in the dark pools of Aristion's eyes—his heart racing.

The moment was alive with a palpable sense of anticipation. The hand that had been touching the side of his face reached behind his head and softly brought it forward, causing their lips to touch. Kallian's entire body tingled, as he closed his eyes and opened his mouth to receive the kiss.

He was in heaven. With their mouths pressed together and their tongues entwined, Kallian lost all sense of time. Nothing existed, save Aristion—the man he loved.

Kallian did not want the kiss to end. He had spent many sleepless nights hoping that his feelings for Aristion would be reciprocated, but had never thought it would come to pass. In fact, he had given up on the idea and had resigned himself to the fact that they would simply be friends.

Aristion released him and stepped back, smiling.

"Come, let's get to the cave. You must be exhausted!"

It was true, every muscle in Kallian's body ached from the ride and he had been awake for hours. He briefly recalled the moment when he had risen with the sun and decided to go hunting—oblivious to the events that were about to transpire.

"Hold a moment!" Kallian exclaimed, the kiss having distracted him from the information he needed to impart.

"Yes, what's up?" Aristion responded, turning towards him, a momentary flash of concern passing across his features.

"Xerxes is camped outside Sardis with a huge army. He's planning to invade Greece!"

"Damn!" Aristion responded with a hiss, causing Kallian to grimace.

For a few seconds there was silence between them in which he appeared to be digesting the news.

Finally, Aristion lifted his gaze and met Kallian's eyes.

"I spotted the campfires, but was not in a position to investigate. Now, it's even more crucial that we reach my contact in Smyrna to arrange passage. I must warn Leonidas."

With a subtle nod toward the trail that wound steeply around the rocky outcrop above them, he added, "There's nothing we can do about it now. Let's keep moving. You must be exhausted."

As they led their horses over the rugged terrain, Aristion glanced back, his expression pensive.

"It's fortuitous our charade held up for as long as it did," he remarked. "Had we been exposed even a day or two earlier, our mission would have ended in failure. It seems we have the favour of the gods on our side."

Kallian smiled, nodding in agreement. Aristion's words resonated with truth. Everything had fallen into place just when they needed it to. Given the looming threat to Greece, their time in Sardis would have come to an end regardless. It was as if fate had orchestrated their departure perfectly.

Chapter Twenty-Six

Aristion

480 BCE

The completion of our journey was marked by the coming dawn, although the rising sun was obliterated by an ominous dark swirl of clouds.

As we made our way along the narrow mountain path to the location of our hideout, a strong wind had materialized. My senses warned me that it heralded the imminent arrival of a huge storm. Due to this, I had increased our pace, since I had no desire to be caught out in the open on a precarious mountain trail. After everything we had been through, the last thing I wanted was to witness Kallian falling to his death.

From my current vantage point, standing in the mouth of the cave, I had a spectacular view of the clouds racing towards us. Dawn had attempted to raise its head but had been extinguished, as if the sun had been eclipsed by the moon. The timing of our arrival was fortuitous, since the weather of the region could be brutal and showed no mercy, especially for the ill-prepared. The wind howled through the mountains, carrying with it the scent of rain and the distant rumble of thunder, a clear sign of the tempest that was about to unleash its fury.

I directed Kallian to tether the horses in a secluded clearing nestled within a natural amphitheater of sorts. The terrain formed a protective barrier, with steep banks rising almost vertically in places, shrouded in dense shrubs and foliage. It was an ideal spot, offering concealment from prying eyes; the horses would remain unseen unless someone ventured directly above their position. Moreover, the abundance of small shrubs and foliage provided ample grazing opportunities, shielded from the impending storm's gusty winds.

Swiftly, I scoured the area for dry wood, making several trips until I had gathered enough to last us through the coming day. The kindling proved to be dry, igniting with ease, and before long, the crackling flames of a roaring fire bathed the rocky walls in a warm, flickering orange glow.

As an added boon, Kallian emerged, laden with an armful of wood he had collected while returning from tethering the horses.

"That was close! All hell is about to break loose out there!" he remarked with a grin, water dripping from his nose and chin.

I couldn't help but smile as I looked up at him. He was truly a sight to behold, almost ethereal in his beauty. The play of firelight on his features only accentuated his allure, and in that moment, I found myself utterly captivated. His presence elicited a feeling of warmth within me, one that had nothing to do with the fire.

As Kallian approached, his smile widened in response to my gaze. With a graceful ease, he set down the wood he had been carrying, the flickering light dancing in his eyes as he closed the distance between us. He stopped directly opposite me, the fire casting a soft glow on his features as he stood, a subtle tension lingering in the air.

With a grin still playing on his lips, Kallian's gaze remained locked on mine as he peeled off the long, wet robe draped over his frame. The attire, typical of most Persians, clung to him, and it was evident he wanted to shed it as quickly as possible. Yet, beneath the surface, his mischievous expression and the glint in his eyes hinted at a motivation that extended beyond the mere discomfort of the wet clothing.

The corners of my mouth turned up into a broad smile.

Standing before me, his bare chest rising and falling with each heavy breath, Kallian locked eyes with me once more, unwavering. In that unbroken gaze, I felt the intensity of his love wash over me like a wave, causing my breath to hitch in my throat and my heart to race.

Without bending over, he kicked off his boots and released the buckle of his wide leather belt. He let it fall to the ground, along with the *shamshir* that was attached to it. The whole time he was in the process of disrobing, his eyes remained transfixed on mine—burning with a mixture of love and unbridled passion.

His hands then moved to the rope tie on his *shalwar's*, and I found myself involuntarily tracking the motion, unable to maintain eye contact.

As he released the knot, the final piece of clothing cascaded to the ground, leaving him completely exposed before me.

Kallian was now standing before me naked, the firelight dancing on his glistening body. His shaft was fully aroused, reaching up to the heavens, obscuring his belly button. As I watched, it pulsated, expanding and contracting with each beat of his heart. My vrykolakas vision even allowed me to take in the bead of white on its head, wet from the flow of life that wanted to explode from him.

Without another thought, I got to my feet and quickly shed my garments. My own manhood, finally free from the *shalvar's* that restrained it, joined Kallian's in its heavenly salute. As I closed the final distance between us, his gaze wandered, exploring every aspect of my body. Finally, his eyes came to rest—meeting mine.

I wrapped my arms around him, pulling his lean, muscular torso close, and brought his lips to mine. As our tongues intertwined in a passionate dance, the exchange was intoxicating. Every sense heightened, every nerve electrified, I felt myself slipping into a blissful state of euphoria, completely lost in the moment.

My hands continued to explore his body, caressing the athletic contours of his back and then came to rest on his well-muscled buttocks. He let out a groan of pleasure as I grasped them tightly—the tips of my fingers digging into his flesh. I pulled him closer still, causing his sizeable manhood to expand and contract as it came into contact with my flesh. It was now pressed against the entire length of my abdomen and was throbbing in unison with his beating heart.

I brought a hand back to his head and entwined my fingers through the strands of his long black hair. As I did so, I reached down and began to run my fingers along the prominent veins of his shaft. Kallian moaned and mirrored the move, grasping my manhood in return.

As he gripped my shaft, rhythmically moving his hand up and down its length, I became lost in the sensation of his caress. Smiling, I closed my eyes—my breath quickening.

Time stretched on, but I no longer felt its passage, as beads of sweat shimmering like diamonds in the firelight, traced paths down our torsos—a testament to the heat of our passion.

It did not take long before the culmination of our fervent exchange brought us to the verge of climax. However, since I was far from wanting it to end, I opened my eyes and placed a hand on his wrist—meeting his gaze.

"Kallian, I love you," I confessed, my voice barely above a whisper.

His smile widened. "I love you too. I have for a while."

I reached behind his head and gently pulled his lips to mine. Without the slightest desire to come up for air, the kiss seemed to last an eternity.

Finally, as our lips parted, I felt the brush of Kallian's cheek against mine as he whispered, "I want to feel you inside me."

I did not respond with words, but instead took him by the hand and led him to the blanket that was laid out before the fire.

Kallian sat down, reclined and reached back with his arms in a languid stretch. As I stood before him, I took in the entirety of his athletic physique. From the contours of his muscular body—glistening with the sweat from our intimate exchange, to the large muscle that curved over his abdomen, he was beautiful.

I fell to my knees, gently lifted his legs over my shoulders and gazed into his eyes. Leaning forward, I brought my lips to his and sensed the rhythmic beat of his heart quicken as I entered him. He let out a brief gasp, his muscles tensing, before he finally relaxed—the corners of his mouth turning up into a blissful smile.

Chapter Twenty-Seven

Kallian

480 BCE

The storm raged the entire day and into the following evening. Even with the need to warn Leonidas, it seemed prudent to wait it out. There was still plenty of time. The army had just arrived in Sardis and would probably be there a few days. Moreover, it would only be able to move at a fraction of the speed they were able to sustain on horseback.

Kallian had welcomed the opportunity to simply be with Aristion, rather than on the road. They made love countless times and spent most of the day and following evening in each other's arms.

However, the day had not been entirely one of pleasure. Amidst their intimate moments, they had engaged in exhaustive discussions about the looming threat posed by Xerxes and Greece's limited options for defending against the vast army aligned against them.

As the hours slipped away, Kallian found himself wishing for time to slow its relentless march. If the circumstances had been different, he would have preferred to revel in the cozy warmth of the fire for days, wrapped snugly in furs beside Aristion. Each moment was precious, and the intimacy shared between them had provided him with a much needed respite from the chaos of the outside world.

~

The next day, Kallian rose early and stepped out of the cave to be greeted by clear blue skies. As he stood there—naked, basking in the rays of the morning sun, he smiled and felt a sense of tranquility wash over him.

Returning to the fire, which had long since died out, he donned some fresh clothes, discarding the military attire he had been wearing when he arrived. Thanks to Aristion's foresight, their hiding place was well-equipped with the necessities of travel: clothes, weapons, and coin.

It was now well past midday, and he was currently riding along a narrow mountain path behind Aristion's white dappled mare. From what Kallian could tell, it looked more like a game trail than a path traversed by the local inhabitants of the area. The choice of route had been necessary, though, to reduce the possibility of encountering patrols. However, due to the terrain, their pace was slow, and it would take them at least another day to reach the port city of Smyrna.

As the journey continued, Kallian's thoughts drifted to the night before. They had made love, then relaxed by the fire in each other's arms, conversing, and then made love again. The evening had been surreal—almost dreamlike. Although he had cared deeply for Eioneus, his feelings for his friend at the *agōgē* had paled in comparison to the love he felt for Aristion.

Truth be told, his mentor had captured his heart during their first few weeks in Sardis. There was something about him that Kallian could not put his finger on, something mystical, almost godlike. In many ways, Aristion reminded him of the descriptions he had read about Ares, the son of Zeus. After watching him fight the clerics, he had even contemplated that Aristion actually was the god of war and courage. This was definitely a conversation he was going to have to have with him. What he had witnessed in Sardis still left him perplexed and defied any form of rational comprehension.

As Kallian continued to ponder, the image of Aristion's face came to mind. His smooth bronze skin, untouched by the passage of time, exuded an air of youth and vitality—leading most casual observers to assume he was barely older than 30. This often worked in his favor, given Aristion's profession, as it led others to underestimate him. However, the deep, emotive pools of his brown eyes radiated a profound level of wisdom, a depth that only came from a lifetime of experience. This was further confirmed by the fact that Aristion had mastered numerous fighting forms and displayed a wealth of knowledge far beyond his years. It would take Kallian the best part of a generation to come close to the mastery displayed by his mentor. Truly, Aristion was the epitome of a paradox—a force of nature where a cloudless sky coexisted with a raging storm.

No matter how hard and long Kallian pondered, there were so many things about Aristion that defied comprehension. However, there was one thing he did know: the love he had for him burned in his heart like the sun as it arced through the heavens.

~

Rounding a bend, the trail before them widened and the expanse of a valley came into view. Kallian let out a sigh of relief. Finally, they were in the foothills of the western reaches of the mountain range that spanned from Mount Tmolus, south of Sardis, to the *Egéo Pélagos*, south of Smyrna.

Taking advantage of the change in terrain, Kallian chivied his horse forward and came alongside Aristion.

"As much as I love the view of the back of your head, I'm relieved we can finally talk!"

Aristion laughed, "Yeah, that was tough. It should be open ground from here out."

Kallian brought his horse closer to Aristion's mare and reached out, placing a hand on his forearm. Aristion glanced over at him, smiled and made eye contact.

"Last night was amazing. I can't stop thinking about it!" Kallian remarked, grinning from ear to ear.

"Me too," Aristion replied, chuckling.

Aristion reigned in his horse, came to a halt and leaned into Kallian, kissing him on the lips. With one hand behind his head and the other on his thigh, he could feel the hard muscle of Kallian's manhood as it snaked down the left side of his *shalvar's* and pressed against the material in an attempt to escape.

Feigning a sigh, Kallian broke contact and glanced down, "Ugh... my shaft has been like that for almost the entire ride! I'm going to need some help after we stop for the night!"

Aristion roared with laughter and with a flourish of a bow replied, "Ok, my love, your wish is my command, but you'll have to hold on for a few more hours!"

"Fine, I'll wait!" Kallian groaned, before glancing at Aristion with a mischievous grin.

Aristion chuckled and then nodded towards a large wooded area on the far side of the valley, "Let's get moving, I want to find some cover before nightfall."

No sooner had their horses lurched into motion and descended into the wide expanse of grasslands, Kallian's thoughts strayed to the subject of Aristion's escape from the clerics. Over the past day there had been numerous occasions in which he had replayed the events in his mind. He desperately wanted answers—something that would help him to make sense of what he had seen. As much as he loved Aristion, he felt that there was a side to him he barely knew.

"Aristion, I wanted to ask you about what happened in the city."

It was almost imperceptible, but Kallian saw a slight tensing of Aristion's muscles. He even closed his eyes briefly, as if he was considering how to respond. Eventually, just as Kallian was beginning to think that he would not answer, Aristion glanced at him.

"Yes, we need to talk, but not now. I'll explain everything after we stop for the night."

Without another word, Aristion looked away, gave the reins of his horse a brief shake and picked up the pace. For now, the conversation was clearly over and Kallian would have to wait.

Chapter Twenty-Eight

Aristion

480 BCE

The sun had slipped below the horizon, casting the world into a tapestry of shadows. Our camp was nestled deep within a heavily wooded area, the only source of light emanating from the small fire crackling before me. Here, surrounded by the cloak of darkness, the likelihood of discovery was slim.

Kallian walked into the glade and dropped a large rabbit next to the fire, smiling.

"It felt good to hunt, but I hate this bow," he remarked with a grimace, casting the weapon aside, along with its quiver of arrows.

"Don't worry, I'll get you a replacement—I know how you loved the last one I gave you."

Kallian grinned, walked over to where I was sitting and gave me a brief kiss, before flopping down beside me.

He soon had the rabbit skinned and impaled on a spit over the fire. As he sat, tending to the cooking meat, he cast a quizzical glance my way, as though on the verge of saying something.

"After dinner," I stated flatly, cutting him off before he had even uttered a word. It was not a conversation I was looking forward to. However, given the turn of events, it had become necessary. If we were going to share a bed, he had to know who I was. Nothing good would come from a relationship based on a lie.

To say I was feeling uncomfortable would be a grave understatement. I was now consumed by a raging torrent of conflicting emotions. Primarily, I grappled with the possibility that he would reject me once he became aware of my vrykolakas nature. Though few knew of our existence, most who did viewed us as demons. The thought caused a tightening in my chest, and I felt a tangible shudder run down my spine. Given the love I felt for him, it was not a scenario I wanted to entertain."

"It's OK, I'm starving anyway," he replied with a shrug. "We can talk after!"

I let out a sigh of relief, laid back, closed my eyes and took comfort in the heat of the fire.

~

"Before I begin, I want you to know that I love you and would willingly give my life to protect you."

"I love you too!" Kallian replied, reaching towards Aristion and grasping his hand.

"I know, but you don't have a complete picture when it comes to me," Aristion grimaced. "Your love for me is based on what you've observed—what I've allowed you to see, not on who I am. You may feel differently once we've talked."

Kallian's expression shifted, a mix of shock and a hint of indignation flitting across his features at Aristion's words.

"What I feel for you is not some childish crush. It's offensive and belittling that you should say such a thing. Good or bad, I love you. No matter what you tell me, my feelings won't change."

"I'm well aware of that. Please don't take offence. Just hear me out."

"OK," he replied with a slight shrug, his attention rapt.

"First off, I want your solemn oath that you won't share what I'm about to say with anyone," I said earnestly, looking directly into his eyes.

He held my gaze, a thoughtful expression on his face. He was obliviously weighing my words carefully, before responding.

"Will keeping my promise to you require me to betray my country?" he queried.

I smiled. This was one of the things I loved about him. Kallian had a keen intelligence and never did anything without weighing up the consequences of his choices.

"It may result in you feeling conflicted, but I promise you that I am completely aligned with Greece and will do everything within my power to ensure that it prevails against the Achaemenid dynasty of Persia."

"That works for me," he responded with a beaming smile. "Honestly, that was the only scenario I could envision posing any challenge to the depth of my feelings for you. And even then, I doubt it would diminish my love for you—though it might have complicated things a little!"

"Well, I guess we'll see! Maybe you need to get a little more imaginative with your deliberations before making such a statement," I chuckled, though the smile didn't quite reach my eyes. I was dreading the conversation I was about to have with him. Although the love we had for each other burned with the strength of The Flame of Olympus, what I had to say was going to be a lot for him to handle, no matter how deep his feelings for me.

Kallian's brow furrowed with concern, and he leaned in slightly. "What is it? You know you can tell me anything. It won't change anything!"

"OK," I grimaced. "Well—I guess my birth is as good a place as any to start. I was born in a small village nestled amidst the rugged terrain of northwestern Greece, just beyond the imposing silhouette of Mount Smolikas," I began, my voice carrying a hint of nostalgia. "Though the exact date of my birth eludes me, it occurred during the waning years of Eurycratides's reign, the thirteenth king of Sparta, just before his son Leon ascended to the throne."

"WHAT?!" Kallian gasped, a look of suspicion on his face. "You are joking, right?"

"No," I responded, flatly.

"But… but…" he stammered, obviously confused. Given the way in which his fingers had begun to move, he appeared to be carrying out some mental arithmetic.

I waited patiently, giving him the time to assimilate what I just told him.

That was over 100 years ago—that can't be right!" he shouted, his voice carrying a blend of disbelief and astonishment. It was as if he had been struck by lightning, his tone rising at least an entire octave. The words tumbled over each other in a rush, as if competing to escape his mouth.

"111 to be exact," I confirmed, levelling my gaze at him.

Kallian's draw dropped, his face displaying a mask of abject disbelief, which quickly turned into a smile, as he began to chuckle. With a feigned scowl, he punched me gently on the shoulder.

"Seriously Aristion, stop messing with me. Just tell me the truth. There's absolutely nothing you can say that will change how I feel about you—I love you!"

"I am telling you the truth," I replied firmly, without even a hint of a smile. Pausing, I took a deep breath. "Kallian, I'm a vrykolakas!"

Kallian looked stunned. His mouth began to open as if he were about to say something, but he ended up shutting it—without so much as a word. He simply sat there, body rigid, a mixture of shock and incredulity evident on his face.

Breaking eye contact, he stared at the fire, lost in thought. It felt like an eternity before he finally glanced up, his eyes carrying a plea, silently reaching out for understanding.

"But Aristion, you can't be a vrykolakas. They aren't real!" he said, a slight tremor in his voice.

"Kallian. I wish that were true, but I am a vrykolakas. Given the fact that I'm sitting right in front of you, I'm living proof that that they exist," I replied, before adding, "well the 'living' part may be up for debate!"

"But I know you. You aren't evil!" he spluttered.

I chuckled, though tinged with resignation. His perspective wasn't surprising; he viewed things in absolutes, devoid of any nuance. The myths, steeped in superstition, had painted my kind in the darkest of hues.

Maintaining eye contact, I smiled in an attempt to reassure him.

"Just because someone is a vrykolakas, doesn't make them inherently evil. Yes, there are a few bad apples among our kind, but that's no different from the world of humanity. Some men are wicked, like the Satrap's nephew, while others are good. Vrykolakas are no different!"

Although it was obvious that Kallian was experiencing a multitude of conflicting emotions, he looked reflective, as he pondered my words.

"You say vrykolakas are no different, but all the accounts I've read describe them as soulless predators. They prey on humans, leaving lifeless corpses in their wake. Aside from their form, they're nothing like us..." His voice trailed off, cracking as he uttered the word 'us', realizing that the term no longer applied to me.

"Kallian, you need to put aside the misconceptions you have about my kind. They are based on fables, not reality."

"So, you don't drink human blood?"

Inwardly, I groaned. This conversation was far from over and was going to require a mixture of patience and deftness on my part.

"Yes, but we don't kill to feed—unless our lives are in danger. I would never take the life of an innocent, any more than you! Some humans willingly offer their blood in exchange for coin. When that's not available, we might take a small amount from a person—along with their memory of the event. They may feel a bit fatigued afterward, but otherwise, they are none the wiser."

Given the expression on his face, my words did not appear to be allaying his concerns. Instead, he looked mortified.

"What?! You take both a person's blood and their memory—without even asking?" he sputtered, the words tumbling from his mouth in horror. "Have you done this to me?"

"No! I would never do that to you!" I replied, firmly. "I've never taken your blood, or influenced your thoughts. You are my friend and I would give my life to protect you!"

He looked directly into my eyes and after a couple of deep breaths, nodded, apparently satisfied.

"I believe you, but I'm struggling to wrap my head around all of this. I thought I knew who you were, but now I see that I was barely scratching the surface."

"So, now that you know, have your feelings about me changed?"

Kallian looked down, closed his eyes and let out a big sigh, before raising his head and meeting my gaze.

"No. I still love you. That said, I do have a lot of questions."

"Anything. Ask away," I responded quickly, relieved by his response. In fact, he was handling the conversation a lot better than expected. My high opinion of him was not misplaced. He truly was exceptional.

"If what you say about vrykolakas is true, why are the stories about them so horrific?"

I grimaced, feeling the weight of his question settle heavily upon me. It was as if I stood at the edge of a precipice, unsure of the depth of the chasm that lay before me.

"As much as I'd like to tell you otherwise, there is a degree of truth to them. After we came into being, the vrykolakas went through a dark age. It lasted almost 200 years. Without the necessary discipline to control our urges, or a governing body to impose laws, we ran rampant, killing indiscriminately. We were like a plague of locusts set loose on the fertile farmland of humanity."

I now had Kallian's complete attention. As he sat in front of me, illuminated by the firelight, he reminded me of an inn patron, sitting in silence, captivated by an engaging yarn being imparted by a storyteller.

"However, our numbers were few and humanity began to fight back, decimating our ranks. It was then that one of our elders, Aegeous, a vrykolakas who lived the life of a hermit, gathered a few survivors and began to train them in the art of restraint. He helped them to master their urge to feed.

It was remarkable what he managed to achieve, since many vrykolakas had little desire to change. That said, without change, the tide of humankind would have swept us from the face of the planet.

Within a few years, the followers of Aegeous numbered around 50 and the vrykolakas council came into being. There were many who encouraged him lead the council—for without him, they would have never reclaimed their humanity. However, he declined, choosing instead to retreat back into his hermitic life."

"What do you mean by 'reclaimed their humanity'." Kallian interjected, obviously enthralled by what I was telling him.

"The vrykolakas I am now, shaped by my sire's training, differs greatly from what I would have become without his assistance. Despite my transformation, I remain, for the most part, the same person I was before I was turned... before I died."

"WHAT! You died?!" he exclaimed, the words bursting from him.

"Yes, the process of becoming a vrykolakas is one of death and rebirth, but I'll get to the later," I responded, holding up my hand to deter further questions.

"The training I received allowed me to gain control over my hunger and retain rational thought, along with my humanity. Due to this, I'm still very much human, no different than you, except for the fact that we require different things to sustain us.

In order for the vrykolakas society to thrive, we have to adhere to rules set forth by the council, the first of which is that no vrykolakas is permitted to exist without training. It is a crime for a vrykolakas to turn someone and leave them untrained. Without this training a fledgling vrykolakas would be at the mercy of its base nature—no better than a rabid animal in search for its next meal."

"You say 'it' like it's an animal, not one of your number."

"It is an animal. In vrykolakas society there is a marked distinction between one who is trained—thereby maintaining their humanity and one that is not."

Kallian nodded in understanding, but given his deeply furrowed forehead and the intense curiosity emanating from his eyes, we still had a long way to go. It was going to be a long night.

"Why are vrykolakas only referred to in fables? No one seems to know about them."

I smiled, greatly encouraged by the balanced and rational nature of Kallian's questioning.

"About 700 years ago, during humanity's attempts to purge us from the earth, they were also embroiled in their own conflicts. Over the course of two centuries, the Mycenaean civilization crumbled, its palaces fell, and trade routes collapsed amid severe droughts, leading to a drastic decline in population.

Few records of vrykolakas existence survived this turbulent era of human history. Since then, we've largely remained hidden, with one notable exception—the Persians. Darius learned of our existence a few years ago and vowed to eradicate my kind. This is one of the primary reasons why the vrykolakas council is committed to ensuring Greece's victory in their war against Persia."

Kallian smiled, obviously pleased that we had a similar goals when it came to the Achaemenid dynasty of Persia.

"When I was at the *agōgē*, I read everything I could lay my hands on about Mycenaen period of Greek history. There were cursory comments about the existence of vrykolakas, but nothing definitive."

"As it should be! We worked hard to purge what records still remained after what people refer to as the dark age came to an end."

Kallian nodded, looking thoughtful.

"I'm curious, where did vrykolakas come from? How did they even come to exist?"

"Honestly, I don't know much about our origins. Out of the original thirty, only three elders are left, and they…"

"What are elders?" Kallian interrupted, his voice tinged with curiosity, cutting through my words before I could finish my sentence.

"Elders were created, rather than sired," I replied, holding up my hand again to forestall any further interruptions. "They refer to their creator as the 'great betrayer', but for the most part, they refuse to talk about it. All I can tell you is that vrykolakas came about around 700 years ago during the times of Heracles. Apart from the three remaining elders, the rest of my kind were not created but turned.

"How is someone turned?"

"By a vrykolaka draining a person until they are on the cusp of death and then feeding them a few drops of their own blood," I replied.

"So, you could turn me, if I so desired?"

"Absolutely not! Only one in fifty survive the process," I retorted, horrified by the direction in which the conversation was going.

Kallian sighed, the sound mingling with the crackling of the fire as he tossed another log onto the flames. He then fell silent, his gaze fixed on the dancing embers, lost in thought. Eventually, his eyes found mine, and we locked gazes in the flickering light.

"Aristion, I want you to know that my feelings for you have not changed, but I'm going to need a little time to get my head around everything you've told me," he said, speaking softly, his words punctuating the tranquil night air.

I nodded in understanding.

"I'm going to take a walk," he continued, his voice devoid of its usual warmth, almost robotic. It was as if he was in a state of shock, his words echoing hollowly in the clearing.

Breaking eye contact, Kallian rose from his place by the fire, its glow illuminating his silhouette as he slung his bow and quiver over his shoulder. With purposeful steps, he disappeared into the enveloping darkness of the forest, the rustle of leaves underfoot marking his departure.

As his figure vanished into the shadows, the glade descended into silence, interrupted only by the occasional hoot of a distant owl.

Chapter Twenty-Nine

Kallian

480 BCE

The following day they broke camp with the coming of dawn. Kallian had not spoken after his return the previous evening and Aristion had not attempted to elicit any form of dialogue with him. It was just as well, since he was still in the midst of processing the conversation from the night before and was attempting to reconcile the reality of Aristion's vrykolaka heritage, with the man who had won his heart.

Everything he had experienced during his time with his mentor, friend and lover had shown him to be the antithesis of the myths surrounding vrykolakas. However, the revelation that Aristion had deceived him about his true nature unsettled Kallian deeply. The man before him now was not the person he thought he had known.

By midafternoon, they reached an intersection, where their trail connected to the main road into Smyrna. Kallian sighed with relief. The journey had been grueling and he was relieved that they were now only a short distance from the city.

Reaching the city gates, they found its guards in the process of searching a cart and in a heated debate with its owner. The timing was fortuitous, since other travelers, like themselves, were able to pass through without incident.

"We don't have far to go," Aristion commented, as he took a street to their right.

The city sprawled out before them, its stone structures rising in varying degrees of grandeur and decay. Magnificent edifices stood proudly alongside dilapidated buildings, their facades weathered by time and neglect. Each street seemed to tell a story of the city's history, with some streets lined by meticulously maintained structures while others harbored abandoned buildings, their empty windows staring blankly back at them.

“What happened to this city?” Kallian queried, finally breaking the silence that had been prevalent for most of their journey.

Aristion was silent for a moment and then let out a sigh.

“What you see now is simply a shadow of its former glory. It was once a splendid city, as evidenced by some of what you see around you, gesturing at a fallen statue. It appeared to be a representation of Zeus, its pieces scattered around the plinth upon which it had stood. However, due to a mixture of pride and the degeneracy of its citizenry, it lost its ability to defend itself against the Lydian expansion and was finally sacked by Alyattes.”

“How long ago?”

“Just over 100 years.”

“And then the Persians?”

“Yes—around 70 years ago.”

Kallian took a few seconds to digest the information, before glancing over a Aristion, his expression quizzical.

"Given its strategic significance, I’m surprised that it’s still so dilapidated. Why didn’t Cyrus or any of his successors rebuild?" Kallian inquired, his gaze sweeping over the crumbling remnants of what had probably once been a majestic structure.

Aristion shrugged, a contemplative expression on his face. "Your guess is as good as mine. They probably had other priorities," he replied, his tone tinged with a hint of speculation.

They then turned onto the main thoroughfare, the road stretching out before them; a bustling artery of commerce and travel. Dust kicked up by hooves and wheels hung in the air, lending an earthy scent to the surroundings. Amidst this lively procession, merchants haggled over prices, their voices carrying over the din of the crowd. Carts, laden with goods of all descriptions, rumbled along the uneven roads, while pedestrians weaved skillfully through the throng, their faces set with determined purpose.

Here and there, travelers on horseback moved with an air of quiet confidence, their mounts picking their way through the crowd with practiced ease. Among them rode Kallian and Aristion, their presence unremarkable amidst the throng of activity that surrounded them; drawing only an occasional dismissive glance from those they encountered.

Aristion halted his horse with practiced ease, gracefully dismounting and gesturing towards a building nestled to their right. Its façade, weathered but sturdy, seemed to exude a timeless resilience in the face of passing years.

"We're here," he announced with a nod, his gaze shifting towards the sign above the door.

Kallian followed his companion's gaze, noting the depiction of a man holding a small two-handled urn adorning the sign. The symbol indicated that their contact was a wine merchant, a fact confirmed by the faint aroma of fermenting grapes wafting from within.

As they stepped inside, the heavy wooden door creaked softly on its hinges, announcing their arrival. Before them was a large man, seated behind a sturdy wooden counter, his form imposing against the backdrop of the room filled to the brim with urns of all shapes and sizes. The shelves lining the walls were like towering monuments, stacked high with these vessels. It was a scene that evoked a sense of awe and wonder, as if they had stumbled upon an ancient treasure trove.

"What can I do for you…" the merchant queried, his voice welcoming, as he started to look up. He froze and his mouth turned up into a broad grin—the fine lines around his eyes creasing as he did so. "ARISTION!"

"Hello, my friend!"

"I can't believe it's you! What's it been? At least fift…" he exclaimed, but stopped before completing the last word, glancing at Kallian.

"It's OK, my companion knows," Aristion responded with a smile, allaying the man's concerns.

"Ah, good good!"

"Kallian, I'd like to introduce you to my old friend Soroush."

The man jumped to his feet and gave Kallian a slight bow, chuckling as he did so.

"Welcome, it's a pleasure to meet you," he exclaimed, before turning back to Aristion. "Old? That's precious coming from someone who has a least twenty years on me!"

"As in the length of our friendship, not your physical age." Artistion groaned, his eyes rolling back in his head. "I see that your humour has not improved—even after fifty years of practice. You are a lost cause!"

The man let out a belly laugh.

Meanwhile, Kallian had simply stood there—speechless. In the span of two days, his entire reality had been turned on its head. Creatures of myth—vrykolakas, had not only become a reality, but he was now face to face with two of them. What was even more confusing was the fact that he had instantly liked Soroush. Yet again, his preconceptions regarding the nature of vrykolakas had been dashed, like a ship thrown upon rocks in a raging storm.

"As much as I'd like to catch up, we have an urgent matter we need to attend to," Aristion continued. "There's a huge invasion force camped outside Sardis, led by Xerxes and bound for Greece."

Soroush did not look overly surprised and simply nodded, a thoughtful expression on his face.

"Follow me," he responded after a brief pause, then turned and strode toward a door at the back of the shop.

It opened into a small garden, overgrown with weeds and surrounded by a waist-high stone wall. From the vantage point it afforded, they could see the city docks and the *Darya-ye Mazandaran*, the shimmering expanse of the Mediterranean Sea stretching out before them.

Kallian's breath caught in his throat. Upon its waters bobbed a fleet of at least 200 *triremes*—warships of the Achaemenid navy. The ships, with their sleek hulls and imposing wooden oars, formed an imposing sight as they rested on the tranquil waters below them, their sails neatly furled against the masts. Each vessel seemed like a dormant beast, waiting patiently for the command to unleash its power against an unsuspecting foe.

"They arrived early this morning."

"Have you been able to glean any information about the fleets intentions?" Aristion queried.

"Only that it will be here for a few days before heading north to Hellespont," Soroush replied, his brow furrowed in concern. "But the scale of this force suggests a significant campaign."

Kallian inclined his head, concern evident on his face.

"That answers the question regarding the army's route," he remarked, his gaze turning towards Aristion. "The narrow straits of the Hellespont will no longer serve as a natural defense for us."

"Agreed," Aristion concurred, without turning his head—his eyes still transfixed on the scene below.

When they returned inside, the mood inside the shop was somber, to say the least.

"We need immediate passage to Greece, if possible."

"Yes, I figured you would. It will only take a few hours to arrange. You can set sail tomorrow," Soroush replied, his eyes reflecting a sense of camaraderie. Then, with a hint of regret, he added, "I wish you could have lingered for a few days; it's been far too long since our last meeting!"

"I know my friend, I know," Aristion responded, his voice heavy.

"Please, feel free to make yourself at home. I should head out," Soroush continued, before letting out a low chuckle. "Given the time of day, my contact won't be hard to find. He tends to frequent only a couple of taverns."

~

A few hours passed and Kallian was now perched on the wall at the far end of the garden. He was in the process of calculating the exact size of the fleet, which had grown by at least another 100 ships since the first time he had seen it.

Soroush and Aristion were inside preparing dinner and catching up. Rather than sitting on the sidelines, he had taken the opportunity to be alone with his thoughts. Between the revelations regarding Aristion's vrykolakas nature and the impending invasion, he had a great deal on his mind.

Someone coughed behind him.

Kallian turned, only to be greeted by a smiling Soroush.

"It's grown in size," he remarked.

Kallian nodded, sullenly.

"Ah well, it's nothing Greeks can't handle—especially if they have time to prepare."

"I hope so. But given the size of Xerxes army, I'm not so sure."

"Don't worry lad, I'm sure it will work out, especially if the Greeks have enough warning."

"I hope so," Kallian responded, not sounding convinced.

"Given the conversation I've just had with Aristion, I sense that something else is also plaguing you."

"What did he tell you?"

"That you've only just found out about who he—my apologies, we are."

"Yes."

"So, how are you doing? I'm sure it's a lot to process?"

"That would be an understatement," Kallian replied, with a strained laugh.

"The only advice I can offer is this. Discard the stories you've heard about vrykolakas. They are not accurate and don't reflect who we are. I can honestly say that Aristion is one of the greatest examples of humanity I've ever met. Not only does he have a high sense of personal integrity, he also has a reverence for life—all life. The fact that he is a vrykolakas changes nothing. He's still that person—the same person you've grown to love and care for."

Kallian sat in silence for a few seconds, before glancing up at Soroush. "Thank you," he responded, smiling warmly.

"You're welcome my lad!" Soroush replied, clapping him on his back. "Anyway, enough of that, it's time for dinner."

The prospect off food elicited a low rumble of appreciation from his stomach. Having barely eaten for days, he was famished.

As they proceeded to walk back into the house, Kallian turned his head towards Soroush, a mischievous glint in his eyes .

"I have to admit, meeting you has definitely helped. I've now met two vrykolakas and neither have attempted to place me on their dinner menu!"

Soroush roared with laughter.

"Well, I've still not told you what I'm planning for tonight!" he replied, still chuckling.

Kallian let out a groan and then proceeded to follow him up the stairs.

Chapter Thirty

Kallian

480 BCE

After rising early and bidding farewell to Soroush, Kallian and Aristion left Smyrna to rendezvous with their transport across the Aegean Sea.

They were now on a cart trail that intersected with the main trade route leading back into the heart of Smyrna. As they ascended a steep incline, Kallian glanced back over his shoulder and could see the densely packed stone buildings of the port city in the distance. Set against the backdrop of the deep blue waters of the *Daryā-ye Motavaset*, it appeared quite beautiful. However, despite the breathtaking geography, the scene was marred by the ominous sight of numerous triremes, signaling the imminent invasion of Greece.

The sun was now at its zenith and the heat was intense. Kallian's clothing was damp from sweat and beads of perspiration ran down his face, the saltiness stinging his eyes. He casually dropped his reigns to brush away the sweat, in an attempt to clear his vision. No sooner than he had done so, a piercing scream shattered the silence, save from the plodding hoofs of their horses.

Aristion immediately signaled for him to stop. However, they had already rounded a bend in the road, revealing the source of the disturbance, which had been hidden by a rise to their left.

A woman and child were perched on a large cart laden with goods. She was standing, brandishing a small dagger and was attempting to ward off two mounted men armed with *shamshirs.*

Quickly assessing the scene, Kallian took in a youth armed with a sword. He was standing beside the body of a man and engaged in combat with another two men, both on foot. They were being egged on by a mounted man who was off to side. He was laughing and appeared to be taking great pleasure in the plight of the travelers they were accosting.

"Bandits," Aristion hissed.

"They have not seen us. Let's pull back and take another route," Kallian responded quickly, keeping his voice low. "Or not," he added under his breath as Aristion responded by kneeing his horse into a gallop, making directly for the cart.

Without another thought, Kallian committed to the course of action chosen by Aristion and took off after him, drawing his *shamshir* as he did so.

Aristion was almost upon them when the bandit who had been laughing screamed a warning to his comrades. He was a middle-aged man with a long, scraggly grey beard, his clothing dirty, faded with age, and in a state of disrepair. He looked determined as he jerked his horse into motion in order to intercept Aristion.

Both of the bandits who were fighting the youth turned simultaneously. It was a mistake. The young man thrust his sword through the back of one and Aristion, who was now upon them, took the head off the other with a single swing of his sword.

Kallian directed his horse toward the three bandits, who were now almost within striking range of Aristion. This caused one of them to break from the group to meet his charge. As the man swung his *shamshir*, Kallian leaned back in his saddle, causing the blade to pass harmlessly over his head. At the same time, Kallian's blade cut deeply into the side of the bandit's torso, causing him to fall from his horse with a dull thud.

Kallian then turned his mare in a tight arc, only to discover that Aristion had already dispatched one of his foes and the last bandit had disengaged; he was attempting to flee. Without hesitation, Kallian sheathed his *shamshir*, took hold of his bow, knocked an arrow, sighted, and let loose. The shaft struck the bandit cleanly between his shoulder blades. The man's head slumped forward, and he toppled from his horse, which continued its frenzied gallop before finally disappearing around the bend in the road.

As Kallian dismounted, he found Aristion kneeling beside the crumpled figure of the fallen man, the youth next to him. The young man, with his long black curly hair framing his features, looked mortified and was clearly in a state of shock.

"Bahram, Bahram," the woman cried as she jumped from the cart and ran to where the prone man lay. "My husband—is he alive?"

"Yes, the wound is deep, but I don't think any major organs have been punctured," Aristion replied, glancing up at the woman. "In fact, I'm not even sure why he's unconscious."

"He fell and struck his head," the youth responded, relief evident in his voice.

"I need some water to clean the wound and cloth to bind it." The woman ran back to the cart, almost tripping in her haste.

"Mama, is daddy OK?" came a little voice from the child, still seated on the cart. She was whimpering and Kallian felt his heart lurch. He could not believe that he had actually suggested leaving these travelers to their plight.

"Yes dear, daddy will be fine," her mother replied, attempting to sound reassuring. However, Kallian could hear a quiver in her voice—reflecting how she truly felt.

Returning with a roll of fabric and an animal skin filled with water, Aristion thanked her and immediately got to work. True to form, he did so with an all too familiar efficiency and expertise.

"OK, this is best I can manage with what we have available. He needs a healer. You are not far from Smyrna and should make haste"

Effortlessly, Aristion picked up the wounded man and began to walk over to the cart, while his wife began to clear a space for him in the back. From what Kallian could see, it was laden with a variety of fabric rolls, varying in texture and colour—the wares of a cloth merchant.

"Thank you, thank you," the woman babbled. "I don't know how we can repay you."

"No need. It was our pleasure to be of assistance," Aristion replied, giving her a warm smile.

The woman threw her arms around him in an embrace, a tear in her eye.

"You are a good man. If only the world had more men like you—it would be a far better place. Thank you!"

With that, they bid farewell and resumed their journey. The rendezvous with their contact was scheduled just after dusk, and they still had quite a distance to cover.

It did not take long for them to crest the mountainous terrain, located on the southern reaches of Smyrna. Aristion glanced over Kallian, to find him staring at him with a quizzical look.

"You are probably wondering why I assisted subjects of our enemy?" he sighed.

"Yes," Kallian replied. "Especially since we need to make haste and avoid attention."

"Firstly, although they are Persian, they are not our enemy. They are simply people who are tied to the geography of their birth. No different than you or me."

"OK, I can see your point," Kallian conceded, recalling his connection with Armeen, the city guardsman. Initially beginning as an intelligence gathering operation, the association had quickly blossomed into a friendship. Over the course of two years, he had idled away many nights drinking with the guardsman—one whose wicked sense of humour had left his belly aching from laughter. There had even been occasions when he had the pleasure of dining with his wife Amaya, who was an excellent cook!

"But why take the risk?" Kallian continued, after a brief pause.

"I am very much the same person I was before I was turned, with the exception of being a little older and wiser."

“A little?” Kallian scoffed, giving him a sidelong glance.

“Point taken—a lot,” Aristion replied with a grin, before continuing.

"After many years of being bullied as a youth and then accosted by bandits, I can't simply sit on the sidelines when others are facing similar dangers. Ultimately, I owe my life to Megareus, who rescued me from a situation much like the one we just experienced."

“Who was Megareus?”

“My master, the vrykolakas who turned me. He saved my life.”

This comment prompted a barrage of questions, which Aristion welcomed. In truth, he felt relieved. The fact that the man he loved was not only conversing but also seemed to be slowly coming to terms with his vrykolakas nature helped ease the tension that had lingered between them since their fireside conversation.

Chapter Thirty-One

Aristion

480 BCE

We arrived at the small bay, our rendezvous point, just before dusk. Our contact was a man called Alborz, a smuggler who was in the employ of the vrykolakas council. He would be meeting us a few hours after dark.

The bay was difficult to access except by sea, providing a natural layer of security. However, according to Saroush, during low tide, it would be possible to navigate around the southernmost cliff face as the water receded to around waist deep.

We only had to wait about an hour before the waters of the *Daryā-ye Motavaset* had dropped to the desired level. With the exception our horses, which we were forced to release from our employ, we were able to traverse the short distance easily.

Finally standing on firm sand, still wet from the retreating tide, I glanced up at Kallian. He had turned and was basking in the last rays of the sun, as it descended beneath the distant horizon.

"I love the sea" he remarked, finally meeting my gaze and smiling.

"Me too. I have a home on the coast in north wester Greece. I'll take you there sometime, if you'd like?"

"Yes, I'd love that!"

Given that he responded without even a moment's hesitation left me both elated and relieved. His immediate warmth and openness were a stark contrast to the coldness I had felt from him over the past few days. This shift in his demeanor was a marked improvement, filling me with hope. His eyes, once distant and guarded, now shone with a newfound connection, and his voice carried a gentle sincerity that had been missing before. This change was not just a relief; it was a rekindling of the bond we shared, bringing a sense of comfort and joy that had seemed out of reach.

The love emanating from him eyes as he looked into my eyes was palpable, as was the quickening of my heart. He then began to close the distance between us and within seconds had wrapped his arms around me in a tight embrace.

"Aristion, I'm sorry it took me so long. Please know that I never stopped loving you. It was just a lot to process!"

I laughed.

"Long?" I replied, a chuckle escaping my lips. "I only told you three days ago! Most people would have run in the opposite direction—let alone have the ability to come to terms with what I am."

"Yes, I guess. But I'm not anyone," he smirked, the corners of his mouth turning up into a mischievous grin. "Anyway, I think it's time for a swim. Want to join me?"

"Sure!"

Immediately, he broke contact and began to strip off his wet clothes, which he gathered and laid out on a nearby rock.

I just stared, taking in the entire length of his glistening body. From the curls of his long black hair—which fell down the contours of his well-defined back, to the rounded muscles of his buttocks, he was beautiful.

Task complete, he turned and without hesitation, broke into a sprint.

"Last one in makes dinner!"

Breaking out of my trance, I didn't even bother to strip. Instead, I immediately drew upon the full extent of my vrykolakas speed. To the naked eye, my form blurred, and within seconds, I was standing in knee-deep water, directly in front of him

He almost fell, as he stumbled to a halt.

"That's not fair! he barked. "Now that I know about you, you're going to be insufferable—I know it!"

"My apologies, I couldn't help myself!" I retorted, laughing. "But I'll make it up to you with dinner!"

"Fine," he grumbled, feigning irritation and pushing against my chest with the palm of his hand.

Still grinning, I leaned in and kissed him briefly on the lips, savoring the moment before stepping around him and heading back to shore. The soft sand shifted under my feet, and the setting sun cast a golden glow on the tranquil scene.

"Take your time; it will be a while before dinner is ready," I remarked, glancing back over my shoulder, catching his eyes one last time.

Behind me, I heard the unmistakable splash as Kallian dove into the warm, crystal-clear waters of the *Daryā-ye Motavaset.*

An hour later, Kallian and I were sitting crossed legged in front of a small fire, eating a stew made of root vegetables and cured meat. He was obviously famished, since he was already mopping up the remains in his bowl with a chunk of bread.

"It's going to be at least another two hours before our boat arrives. I'll keep watch, if you want to get some sleep"

"Nah," he replied. "I'm not in the mood to sleep."

With that, he got up and walked around the burning embers of the fire, the shimmering orange glow of its light, glinting in his eyes.

He knelt, straddling the sides of my crossed legs with a fluid grace, his thighs brushing against mine. As he slowly lowered his buttocks, they gently came to rest on my feet, the warmth of his skin radiating through me. The intimate proximity allowed me to feel the subtle shift of his muscles, his every movement deliberate and tender. The weight of his body, combined with the gentle pressure on my feet, created a sense of closeness that was both comforting and electrifying.

As Kallian gazed into my eyes, I felt the tension I had been feeling since our exit from Sardis dispel, like the darkness of night, under the rays of the morning sun.

"I love you!" he whispered.

"I love you too," I responded, my senses picking up the sound of his heart as its rhythmic beat quickened.

His silhouette was now outlined against the flickering flames, his features veiled in darkness. Yet, he drew nearer, his presence enveloping me, and I caught the scent of the sea lingering in the tangle of his hair. As our lips met, I closed my eyes, losing myself in the intoxicating union of our tongues, a moment of pure bliss amidst the dancing shadows.

Locked in a passionate embrace, our mouths melded together, igniting a fire that consumed us both. In that moment, everything else melted away into oblivion, leaving only the intense connection between us. Time lost its meaning as we clung to each other, our hearts beating as one.

Eventually, our lips parted, but the hunger remained. I yearned for more, craving the closeness that only he could provide.

He rose to his feet with a determined grace, his hands moving to unbuckle the clasp on his *sarband.* The fabric slipped through his fingers, cascading to the ground in a fluid motion, soon joined by his cream-colored *shalvars.* His disrobing was swift, driven by the intensity of our desire, and in mere seconds, he stood before me, bare and unguarded. The evening light played on his skin, highlighting the contours of his body. The air seemed to thicken with anticipation, every moment charged with the electricity of our longing.

Instinctively, my gaze was drawn to his shaft , which was now fully hard—a number of pronounced veins clearly visible along its length. It curved up from a mass of black curly hair at his groin, to a point just above his belly button. It was pulsating rhythmically, in time with the beats of his racing heart.

I walked towards him, placed a hand behind his head and drew his mouth to mine. As our tongues touched, I grasped the hard muscles of his rounded buttocks and pulled him closer still. I did so with such force that his feet lost contact with the ground and he was forced to wrap both of his arms behind my back in an embrace.

Our lips broke contact and he looked into my eyes. Within their depths burnt a passion. One of desire. One of love.

"Take off your clothes off!" he demanded, his tone baulking no argument—not that I would have objected.

"As you command," I replied, a wry smile playing at the corners of my mouth.

Dropping the last of my garments to the sand, I took in the entirety of his body as he reclined on a blanket beside the fire. From the rippling muscles of his abdomen, partly obscured by sheer size of his manhood, to the finely chiseled features of his face, framed by a mop of black curly hair, he was stunning.

I knelt, a knee on each side of his tight waist and felt the entire length of my shaft brush against his, like swords engaged in a duel for dominance. Leaning forward, our mouths touched. Lips parting, we kissed.

In mere moments, we became a tangle of limbs, consumed in the throes of passion. Our lips remained locked, never breaking contact as we rolled together, our bodies intertwined, hands roaming in a fervent exploration of each other.

Placing my palms on his chest, I pushed myself up and lifted his legs over my shoulders. Holding them in place with one arm, I took hold of my manhood and guided its head towards the pink opening between the muscular cheeks of his buttocks.

I was in a state of euphoria—every nerve of my body tingling in anticipation, as I entered him. I felt my shaft swell, as the muscles of his sphincter tightened, causing him to groan—a slight flash of pain passing across his features. I paused, not wishing to cause him discomfort.

Pulling back, I began to softly caress the tight ring of pink flesh with the head of my manhood, causing it to expand and contract, begging to be satiated; to be fulfilled. He moaned, this time in pleasure.

Slowly, for a second time, the tip of my shaft passed from sight. This time, it was met with only a fleeting resistance before he finally relaxed. With closed eyes, his head fell back, and his long black hair unfurled across the sand, framing the chiseled features of his face.

Wrapping my arm around the back of his neck, I lifted his face to mine and with a gentle thrust of my hips, the entire length of my manhood disappeared from view, eliciting another gasp. As I did so, I felt his entire body go taut and his nails dig into the skin of my back.

With the side of his face pressed against mine, I began to bite his neck, being careful not to break the skin, while my hips fell into a rhythmic pattern, my shaft expanding and contracting with each thrust.

The connection I felt with Kallian went way beyond the physical sensation of being entwined in the throes of passion, or the heat of his flesh against my shaft—which was now deep within him. There was no longer any sense of separation. We were one breath. One heart. One soul.

Still holding the back of his head with one hand, I grasped the hard pulsating rod between his legs with the other. My fingers encircled it at the base, the tips barely touching and then began to move my hand up and down its entire length.

The pace of my thrusts quickened and I could feel his grip tighten—his breathing mirroring each movement of my hips. Quicker. Quicker. Quicker.

With his mouth pressed against my ear, the loud roar that escaped his mouth almost deafened me. His spine arched, causing him to fall back onto the sand, breaking my hold on his head. Body spasming, a huge fountain of white exploded from the head of his shaft, covering the entire length of his torso—even reaching his face. Again and again, he spasmed and each time a stream of pearls broke forth, although lessening with each release.

It was as if Kallian's orgasm had ignited something in me. With one final deep thrust, I felt the already swollen veins of my manhood expand and stretch, almost to breaking point. I could no longer contain it—not that I had any desire to. My manhood erupted. It did so with such intensity that I threw back my head and screamed.

On the cliffs above us, three birds that had been resting in a shrub, squawked and took to the air—not that I had enough mental faculty left to notice.

Chapter Thirty-Two

Kallian

480 BCE

The small merchant vessel, its wooden hull weathered by years of voyages across the Aegean Sea, arrived silently, its sails billowing in the dying light of the sun as it dropped below the horizon. The crimson hues of dusk painted the sky, casting an ethereal glow upon the waters below.

Promptly, a small rowboat was dispatched from the ship's side, gliding effortlessly over the calm waters towards where they waited on the shoreline. The rhythmic sound of oars dipping into the sea echoed softly in the evening air as they approached.

As they boarded the vessel, the crew worked swiftly, their movements practiced and efficient. The ship wasted no time in setting sail, eager to depart from the shores under the control of the Achaemenid Empire and return to the safety of Greek waters. The captain, his gaze steely and determined, spared no moment in charting their course, since his entire focus was on navigating away from enemy territory.

As the coastline disappeared from view, Artistion turned to Kallian, "Let's get some rest, it's been a long day and I'm sure you are exhausted."

"Yeah," Kallian responded with a yawn, stretched out his arms and let out his breath with an audible exhale. He then looked at Aristion quizzically, "You aren't tired in the least, are you?"

"No."

"Do you ever sleep? Really sleep?"

"No," Aristion replied with a grimace, knowing what was about to come.

"So, all those times you told me you were retiring, you weren't?"

“No, not really," Aristion admitted with a hint of mischief in his tone.

“What did you do then?”

"I read," Aristion replied casually, a faint smirk playing on his lips. "Well, mostly."

“And on other occasions?”

"I climbed out the window to go reconnaissance," he confessed, the smirk growing wider as he recalled his exploits.

Kallian rolled his eyes and sighed, a mixture of exasperation and fondness evident in his expression.

“OK, I’ve heard enough. I don’t care what the risk is, I want you to turn me!”

“ABSOLUTELY NOT!” Aristion responded, his tone brooking no argument.

~

An entire day had now passed, and the small merchant vessel was still cutting through the waves of the *Darya-ye Mazandaran*, its sails billowing in the wind as it made its way towards the shores of Greece. Onboard, Kallian stood at the railing, gazing out at the expanse of water that stretched out before him, the horizon merging seamlessly with the sky.

Despite the urgency of their mission to warn the Spartans about Xerxes' impending invasion, Kallian found himself lost in thought. The rhythmic lapping of the waves against the hull provided a soothing backdrop to his contemplations. He couldn't shake the weight of his concerns about his relationship with Aristion. His refusal to turn him into a vrykolakas, despite his request, gnawed at him like a persistent ache.

As the sun dipped towards the horizon, casting a golden hue over the sea, Kallian's mind wandered further into the realms of uncertainty. He wondered about the future, about the toll that time would inevitably take on their bond. Would Aristion remain forever youthful, while he aged and eventually withered away? The thought sent a shiver down his spine, mingled with a sense of resignation.

He turned at the sound of footsteps and caught sight of Aristion striding purposefully across the deck, his movements fluid and decisive. Despite the gravity of their situation, he seemed unfazed, his steely resolve unwavering. Kallian couldn't help but admire Aristion's strength, both physical and mental. As a vrykolakas, Aristion possessed a power and vitality that seemed to emanate from his very being, a stark contrast to the limitations posed by both Kallian's humanity and mortality.

"You seem quieter than usual," Aristion remarked, his brow furrowing with concern. "Is everything alright?"

Kallian hesitated for a moment, his gaze fixed on the horizon before offering a vague response. "Just lost in thought, I suppose. It's nothing."

Aristion studied Kallian, sensing that there was more to his silence than he was letting on. However, despite his curiosity, he chose not to press the matter. Kallian would share when he was ready.

With a gentle smile, he rested a comforting hand on Kallian's shoulder, a silent yet profound gesture of reassurance. Together, they stood side by side, their figures silhouetted against the backdrop of the setting sun. In that shared moment, amidst the tranquil beauty of the evening, they found solace in each other's presence, drawing strength from the unspoken bond that bound them together.

Chapter Thirty-Three

Kallian

480 BCE

Aristion and Kallian stood outside the grand doors of the throne room of King Leonidas in the heart of Sparta. The walls of the corridor were adorned with magnificent tapestries, their vibrant colors contrasting with the somber stone. Torches lined the hallway, casting flickering shadows that danced across the marble floor.

The two Spartan soldiers stationed at the entrance to the chamber resembled unyielding statues, their presence alone a formidable display of Spartan discipline and strength. Their bronze armor caught the flickering torchlight, casting a subtle gleam across the chamber. Each held a spear with a firm grip, a silent testament to their unwavering readiness to defend their king at a moment's notice.

As Aristion and Kallian approached, a third guard emerged from the throne room, his demeanor stern and focused. He fixed them with a steely gaze before speaking in a firm tone. "The king was appraised as your arrival and will see you immediately," he announced, his voice echoing in the corridor.

With a nod from the two guards standing sentry, Aristion and Kallian entered the room.

The chamber spoke volumes of Spartan power, its walls adorned with intricate carvings and its floor polished marble, each detail resonating with Spartan prestige and influence. At the far end, King Leonidas occupied a high-backed chair, its sturdy oak frame bearing the weight of history. He appeared to be scrutinizing a document, which he set aside before looking up to acknowledge their presence.

"Aristion, my old friend," he said, his tone carrying genuine warmth. "It's good to see you again."

Aristion reciprocated with a respectful bow, a genuine smile adorning his face. "Likewise," he replied, his demeanor reflecting both reverence and camaraderie.

He then inclined his head towards Kallian, before continuing.

"Your Majesty, permit me to present Kallian. He has proven himself an invaluable asset in our endeavors in Sardis, demonstrating remarkable courage and resourcefulness. He is an unparalleled testament to Spartan training and discipline."

King Leonidas, his discerning eye piqued by Aristion's commendation, turned his gaze toward Kallian. "Your dedication to Sparta is noted and valued," he remarked graciously.

"And it was not just his skills regarding information gathering that proved invaluable," Aristion added, a note of pride in his voice. "During our hurried escape from Sardis, Kallian risked his own life to save mine. Without his quick thinking and bravery, I may not be standing before you today."

Leonidas glanced back at Kallian, a broad smile spreading across his face. In three strides, he had crossed the distance to where Kallian stood and grasped him, placing a hand on each shoulder.

"You have earned both my respect and gratitude for your actions. Sparta is truly fortunate to count you among its defenders," Leonidas declared warmly.

Kallian's chest swelled with pride, his resolve strengthened by the acknowledgment of his bravery. With a respectful bow, he expressed his thanks to King Leonidas. "Thank you, Your Majesty."

Once the pleasantries were exchanged, Aristion wasted no time in delivering the grim news of the Persian threat.

"Your Majesty, a Persian army of 100,000 men led by Xerxes is about to cross the narrow stretch of water at Hellespont. The invasion of Greece is imminent!"

There was a tense pause as Aristion's words sank in, casting a shadow over the room. Leonidas's expression darkened, and he clenched his jaw in frustration.

"By the gods," he muttered, his voice laced with concern. "There is not enough time to gather our forces. How long do I have?"

"A week at most," Aristion replied.

Leonidas nodded thoughtfully, his brow furrowed in concentration, before striding purposefully over to a map spread out on a stone table to the left of his throne. With deliberate movements, he traced his finger along the coastline, studying the terrain intently. His expression remained grave yet resolute as he assessed the pros and cons of the various strategic options available to him.

"Here," he declared, his voice resonating in the chamber. "We will hold them at Thermopylae."

"Excellent," Aristion agreed, his smile grim. "The narrow pass at Thermopylae would be my choice too. It presents an opportunity, given the limited number of troops you'll have at your disposal. Your sole chance lies in preventing Xerxes from unleashing the full extent of his force.

~

Aristion and Kallian were now relaxing in the warm waters of the royal bathhouse, situated in the palatial west wing of King Leonidas' residence. After their grueling journey from Sardis, it was a much-needed and well-deserved respite, offering Aristion the chance to speak with Kallian about what had been troubling him.

The building was a testament to Spartan grandeur. Upon entering, one was immediately struck by the opulence within. Towering marble columns supported a vaulted ceiling adorned with exquisite frescoes depicting scenes from Spartan mythology—a marvel of architectural prowess.

At the heart of the bathhouse lay a colossal pool, its waters shimmering in the soft glow of oil lamps lining the walls. The air was heavy with the scent of aromatic oils and fragrant herbs, enhancing the luxurious atmosphere. Marble benches encircled the pool, offering seating for those who wished to relax and converse while they bathed. Intricately carved statues of Spartan heroes stood at each corner, their stern visages a reminder of the city's martial prowess. Altogether, the bathhouse exuded an aura of majesty and refinement, befitting the stature of King Leonidas and his esteemed guests.

As Aristion reclined with Kallian in the warm water, he couldn't ignore the heavy silence that lingered between them. Concern gnawed at him as he tried to decipher the thoughts behind Kallian's furrowed brow.

"Kallian," he began, the words escaping before he could hold them back. "I know something is wrong. What's troubling you?"

Kallian glanced up, surprise flickering in his eyes before uncertainty clouded them. "It's nothing, Aristion. Just lost in my thoughts." The same answer he had given on the boat.

But Aristion knew him too well to accept the deflection. "It's about my refusal to turn you, isn't it?" he pressed gently.

Kallian hesitated, then nodded, his gaze dropping to the water. "I can't shake the feeling that I'm holding you back," he admitted, his voice barely above a whisper. "That I'll never be able to match you in combat, never be your equal."

Aristion's heart clenched at his words, the weight of Kallian's insecurities hanging like a storm cloud between them. "Kallian, you are more than enough," he responded earnestly, reaching out to touch his arm. "You are strong, brave, and resourceful—more so than any human I've ever met. You don't need to become a vrykolakas to be worthy of me."

Kallian met his gaze, his eyes almost pleading for reassurance.

"But don't you see, Aristion?" he insisted, desperation creeping into his voice. "With you immortal and me mortal, how can it ever work between us? I'll grow old while you remain forever young."

Aristion sighed, feeling the weight of Kallian's words settle over him like a heavy cloak. "I understand, Kallian; I truly do," he said softly. "But becoming a vrykolakas is not the answer. It's a risk I'm not willing to take."

Kallian looked away, frustration etched into his features. "I know," he murmured, resignation heavy in his voice.

Aristion reached out, cupping Kallian's face and drawing his gaze back. "I love you," he said firmly, pouring all the sincerity he could muster into his words. "And I would rather share this time with you, mortal as you are, than risk losing you entirely in a dangerous transformation."

Kallian leaned into his touch, a small smile tugging at the corners of his lips. "I love you too," he whispered, his voice filled with longing.

And as they sat there, bathed in the warm glow of flickering torches, Aristion felt a new determination form within him. He had to find a way forward in this dilemma. The answer, he knew, lay with Megareus, the vrykolakas who had turned him.

Chapter Thirty-Four

Kallian

480 BCE

As Aristion and Kallian marched alongside King Leonidas and 7,000 warriors, a tangible aura of solemn determination hung in the air. The narrow gorge rose like a titan before them, its towering cliffs and jagged rocks both majestic and forbidding. The sheer steepness of the slopes offered both strategic advantage and formidable defense, creating a natural chokepoint that would funnel any approaching enemy into a narrow corridor of death.

Taking their positions within the pass, the air crackled with tension and anticipation. The rhythmic thud of marching boots echoed off the canyon walls, a steady cadence that mingled with the murmurs of prayer and the sharp clang of shields being readied for battle.

For two relentless days, the clash of swords and the thunder of hooves echoed through the gorge as the Spartans stood firm against the unyielding tide of Persian invaders. The metallic symphony of battle mingled with the anguished cries of the fallen, creating an eerie cacophony that seemed to reverberate off the cliffs surrounding them.

As dusk descended on the evening of the second day, a heavy silence settled over the battlefield like a shroud. Aristion stood amidst the aftermath of the fierce struggle, his breath heavy with exhaustion and relief. The fading light of the setting sun cast long, ominous shadows over the landscape, stretching across a sea of fallen warriors and shattered standards. It was a haunting landscape of both sacrifice and defiance; a solemn testament to the unyielding spirit of those who fought to defend their homeland.

~

The Spartan camp, nestled within the confines of Thermopylae's narrow pass, was now enveloped in a cloak of darkness, save for the flickering glow of torches that dotted the perimeter.

The air was heavy with the scent of sweat and iron, punctuated only by the murmur of voices, hushed and solemn, and the occasional clink of armor as warriors moved about their tasks.

Aristion, Kallian, and King Leonidas sat together at a makeshift table, the flickering light of torches casting dancing shadows around them. Arrayed before them was a modest spread of cured meats and stale bread, the humble fare of warriors on campaign.

As they ate, the three exchanged stories of the day's successes on the battlefield, each tale suffused with a blend of triumph and solemnity. King Leonidas's eyes gleamed with pride as he recounted the valor displayed by his warriors, remarking that the battle had exceeded even his most hopeful expectations.

Just as they were finishing their meal, their conversation was abruptly interrupted by the arrival of a soldier, his breath ragged and his uniform stained with blood. With a sense of urgency, he delivered grave news to King Leonidas—that they had been betrayed by a local resident who had revealed a secret mountain path to Xerxes, putting the Greeks at risk of being outflanked.

A somber silence descended over the group as the weight of the soldier's words sank in. King Leonidas's expression darkened with grim resolve as he turned to Aristion, his voice low and steady.

“Well, my friend, it looks like I spoke too soon about our ability to hold the pass. We are now facing circumstances that are untenable. The battle is lost.”

Leonidas paused, his brow furrowed in contemplation as he appeared to be weighing the gravity of the situation. After a long period of silence that appeared to stretch out into the night, he finally spoke again, his voice steady but tinged with somber resolve.

"Listen carefully, we have been dealt a heavy blow tonight, one that threatens to undo all that we have fought for. But we Spartans do not cower in the face of adversity. We adapt, we overcome, and we emerge stronger for it."

Aristion nodded, his eyes fixed intently on Leonidas, waiting for him to continue.

"Although defeat is inevitable," Leonidas continued, his gaze scanning the faces of those gathered around him, "we can hold our position long enough to allow the bulk of the army to retreat safely."

Aristion's heart sank at the weight of Leonidas' words, but he knew the truth in them.

"And so," Leonidas concluded, his voice ringing with authority, "I will take three hundred of my finest warriors, along with however many Thespians wish to join us, and we will hold this pass until our last breath."

As Leonidas's words hung in the air, Aristion walked over to where he stood and placed a hand on his shoulder.

"You won't be doing this alone; I will stand with you!"

"Thank you, my friend," Leonidas responded, his voice almost a whisper.

Kallian, who had been silent up to this point, walked to their side, his expression resolute. Aristion recognized the look of determination in his eyes and knew what was coming before he even opened his mouth.

"I will stay too!"

"No, absolutely not!"

"But … but …"

"NO!"

King Leonidas held up his hand, motioning for silence. "Aristion is right," he began, his voice carrying authority. "He has spoken highly of your skills during your mission to Sardis. Your role was not just integral; it was exceptional. Without your presence, it would have failed."

Kallian's expression softened slightly. This was high praise coming from the king.

"I understand your reluctance to leave," Leonidas continued, his tone empathetic. "But your death at the pass would be a pointless waste of your talents, talents that Greece desperately needs. That's why I have a different mission for you."

Kallian, whose shoulders had been slumped, immediately stood erect. There was even a slight glint of excitement in his eyes.

"Instead of leaving with the bulk of the army, I want you to use your skills of subterfuge. Hide in the mountains, observe the battle, and then catch up with General Pausanias to give him a detailed report."

Aristion breathed a quiet sigh of relief, recognizing the true intent behind the mission. The outcome of the upcoming battle was both inevitable and predictable. There would be nothing Kallian could tell Pausanias that he would not already know. King Leonidas was simply saving Kallian from certain death. He looked over at his friend Leonidas and gave him a slight nod of appreciation, which the king returned with an almost imperceptible dip of his head."

~

As the majority of the army departed the camp, led by General Pausanias, a solemn atmosphere settled over the remaining 300 Spartans and the 700 Thespians who had volunteered to stay. The mood was heavy with the knowledge that the following day would most likely result in their deaths.

The night was quiet, save the low murmur of distant voices, punctuated by the occasional clink of armor and the shuffle of feet. Aristion and Kallian stood together on a small outcropping of rock, overlooking the camp below.

Finally, Kallian broke the silence, his voice tinged with concern. "Aristion, I can't shake this feeling of dread. I fear for your safety tomorrow."

Aristion turned to Kallian, his tone earnest. "I appreciate your concern," he said, placing a comforting hand on Kallian's shoulder. "But if anyone can get through the upcoming battle, it's me. You, of all people, know how difficult it is to kill a vrykolakas," he added, a smirk twitching at the corner of his mouth. "That's precisely why I don't want you to participate. I'm confident in my ability to survive the day's events, but I would have little desire to live if you perished."

Kallian nodded, his face still solemn. "Yes, I know you are resilient. Killing you is harder than trying to slay a hydra with a blunt knife. Yet, I can't shake this feeling of dread. What if the Persians have a *mágos* in their ranks?"

"I'm pretty sure they don't. Before leaving Sardis, the intelligence I gathered placed them elsewhere. Soroush confirmed this when we met with him. My kind goes to extreme lengths to remain informed about the movements of the Persian *mágos*. Our survival depends on it!"

Kallian nodded almost imperceptibly, but the expression on his face betrayed the fact that he was not convinced.

Aristion smiled reassuringly. "Let's not dwell on what might happen tomorrow," the cadence in his voice lightening, obviously in an attempt to ease the tension. "There's something else we need to talk about."

Kallian looked at him curiously, waiting for him to continue.

"A few years ago," Aristion began, "my mentor Megareus told me about one of the three surviving vrykolakas elders, Lycurgus. According to him, Lycurgus fell in love with a mortal woman. They are both still alive, living in seclusion."

"So, how does that help us?" Kallian queried, looking a little perplexed.

"They fell in love three centuries ago!" Aristion responded in a flat tone, before the corners of his mouth turned up into a wry smile.

Kallian's eyes widened with excitement as he grasped the full implications of Aristion's words. "Do you think we could find them?" he asked eagerly.

Aristion nodded. "If we get through tomorrow, it's worth a try. Perhaps there's a chance to find a solution to your desire to become a vrykolakas after all. That said, please don't set your hopes too high. Most of what I just told you is based on rumour. No one knows for sure."

With a glimmer of hope in his eyes, Kallian turned his gaze back to the camp below. Taking a deep breath, he let it out in a long sigh. No matter the challenges the coming dawn might bring, he was now ready to face them.

Chapter Thirty-Five

Aristion

480 BCE

As King Leonidas surveyed the horizon, I stood by his side, absorbing the sheer magnitude of our challenge. Our eyes met, reflecting a mutual understanding—a blend of resolute determination tinged with a stark recognition of the daunting odds against us.

Leonidas's voice, low and resonant, broke the heavy silence. "Even the gods might hesitate at the sight of such numbers," he said quietly, his eyes never leaving the sprawling enemy lines. "Yet, our duty to Sparta, to all of Greece, compels us to stand our ground. Though today might mark our end, our sacrifice will not be in vain. We must hold them back as long as possible."

I nodded slowly, the gravity of his words sinking in. Before us, the Persian army stretched vast and formidable, an endless tide of warriors that filled the horizon. Their armor shimmered under the fierce sunlight, and the rhythmic march of countless boots sent a tremor through the ground—a foreboding drumbeat of the imminent clash.

Suddenly, the Persian army halted. The air thickened with tension, palpable even from a distance. In a swift, coordinated maneuver, Persian archers surged from the rear to the front lines, their figures stark against the dusty terrain.

Responding with practiced precision, the Greeks quickly formed a tight phalanx. "Advance!" Leonidas bellowed, his command echoing off the nearby cliffs.

His words instantly galvanized his warriors into a solid front, pushing forward to meet the enemy. This proactive advance was crucial; maintaining a static position under the relentless barrage would offer no advantage.

As the archers released their arrows, the air filled with the menacing hiss of the deadly volley, aimed to disrupt and weaken Leonidas's forces. Yet, as our phalanx advanced, the shields overlapped tightly, forming an almost impervious wall against the incoming arrows, allowing us to close in with minimal losses.

Forced to withdraw, the archers hastily retreated behind the safety of their main army. The two forces collided like opposing waves in a violent storm, the impact sending tremors through the battlefield. The clash of swords and the cries of battle echoed through the narrow pass, each reverberating sound intensifying the fierce struggle—a brutal symphony of iron, determination, and the unyielding spirit of men fighting for their homeland.

Despite being vastly outnumbered, the Greeks beside me fought with fierce resolve, driven by desperation and an unwavering commitment. Their eyes burned with fiery determination, and every swing of their swords was fueled by an indomitable will.

It was more than just a battle for survival; it was a profound display of valor and sacrifice. Each warrior fought not only for his own life but for the lives of his comrades, the honor of his family, and the future of his homeland. Throughout the chaos, the extraordinary prowess of Leonidas's warriors shone through, their discipline and training evident in every push they made into the Persian ranks.

In the midst of the Persian combatant's, Leonidas fought with a relentless ferocity. His armor was now stained with the blood of countless foes, and his eyes burned with an unwavering determination. He cleaved through the Persian frontline, a force of nature on the battlefield. However, the sheer numbers began to take their toll, causing him to stumble. Surrounded by a sea of enemies, the once-mighty King of Sparta fell—his sacrifice becoming a rallying cry for the remaining Spartans.

I was with the small number who remained, 20 all told. We let out a roar and launched ourselves into the Persian horde. My movements were a blur, a dance of death that left the enemy sprawled in my wake. With each swing of my sword, I left a trail of severed limbs and spilled entrails. The ground beneath me was slick with blood, making every step treacherous, but my supernatural agility allowed me to navigate the battlefield with lethal precision.

One by one, my fellow Spartans succumbed to the overwhelming numbers. The narrow pass at Thermopylae had transformed into a somber field of the fallen, and finally, I stood alone—the last defender against the tide of Xerxes' forces.

Persian arrows filled the air, a relentless hail seeking to pierce my undead flesh. I moved with a speed that defied mortal comprehension, but it was not enough to escape completely unscathed. While many arrows whizzed past, a few found their mark, embedding themselves in my left arm and back. Yet, with each wound, I regenerated almost instantly, as I pulled the shafts from my body and continued to advance—an indomitable presence amid the chaos.

My eyes burned with a crimson glow as I surveyed the carnage. The Persians, once confident in their overwhelming numbers, now hesitated. Fear crept into their eyes as they beheld the lone vrykolakas decimating their ranks.

In the midst of the enemy, I faced a group of Immortals, the Persian elite. Adorned in gilded armor, their commander emerged, a formidable man that sought to bring an end to my defiance. Our swords met in a clash that reverberated through the pass. However, my blade soon found its mark, piercing through a chink in his armor. A spray of blood marked his demise, and the once-proud leader crumpled to the ground.

As the sea of Persians pressed on, my supernatural resilience finally began to waver—the grotesque spectacle of arrows protruding from my body bearing witness to the toll exacted by the relentless assault.

The Persians, sensing an opportunity, closed in with a renewed sense of purpose. They were driven by a collective desire to overcome the seemingly invincible foe that stood before them. As the relentless tide reached its peak, I finally succumbed, falling to one knee and then to the ground. The world around me dimmed, and the echoes of the fallen Spartans and the battle cries of the Persians gradually faded into an eerie silence. With a heavy heart, I closed my eyes, surrendering to the encroaching darkness.

In that fleeting moment before the veil of unconsciousness enveloped me entirely, my last thoughts clung to the love I harbored for Kallian. In the silence that followed, his name echoed like a distant refrain, a poignant melody that accompanied me into the abyss.

Chapter Thirty-Six

Aristion

480 BCE

“Aristion, stop! That’s enough! ARISTION!”

The sharp cry cut through the fog of my consciousness like a knife. As awareness seeped back, the metallic taste in my mouth and the warm, pulsing sensation at my lips ignited a dreadful realization. My heart sank—I was drinking blood, Kallian's blood.

I wrenched my eyes open, only to meet his tormented gaze, the vibrant life in his eyes, usually so full of energy and resolve, dim due to the sheer magnitude of blood loss. Horror clawed at my throat as I released his wrist, falling backward.

"Kallian!" My voice broke, raspy and strained. "What have I done?"

He slumped to the ground, his complexion ghostly, a stark contrast to his usual vigor. "You lost control, Aristion," he gasped, his breathing labored. “But I had to try—I had to bring you back."

My body throbbed with pain from the battle, each beat a grim reminder of the desperate struggle I had just endured. The last remnants of my memory were of me standing alone among the dead and striving single-handedly to hold the pass against insurmountable odds.

"Kallian, I'm so sorry. I never meant—never thought..." My words trailed off, choked by the gravity of my actions.

A weak smile touched his lips as he reached out, his hand shaky but his grip firm. "It’s okay, I’ll be fine.”

Breaking eye contact, I surveyed the grim aftermath of the battle sprawled across the pass of Thermopylae. The ground was littered with the remnants of the fallen—Greek and Persian alike.

"Did you have a clear view from your hiding place?" I asked, my voice strained, as I leaned back against a rugged outcrop of stone, blood seeping from my wounds. They were healing quickly, but were so numerous that even with the magic invested in me by my vrykolakas nature, it would take time.

"There," Kallian responded, pointing. "On a narrow ledge, high up on the cliff face."

I turned my head, following the line of his finger and immediately located where he had been sequestered for most of the day. From his vantage point, he would have had a panoramic view of the battlefield.

Kallian continued, his voice a poignant blend of sorrow and admiration. "I could see everything. The fall of King Leonidas, surrounded and overwhelmed by a tide of Immortals. His final moments were a sight that will haunt my dreams forever."

Vivid images flooded my mind as he described the scene. The battlefield, now eerily silent, was stained with the blood of countless warriors, and the smell of death lingered in the air—a haunting reminder of the brutal conflict that had taken place.

"And then, I saw you. Your final stand was something else—almost surreal. You were a blur on the battlefield, moving so swiftly it seemed as though you were vanishing and reappearing among different groups of enemies. It was as if you were everywhere at once."

His voice held a trace of awe before he looked down, his expression pained. "But the sheer number of them, Aristion. Even with your incredible speed, the odds were stacked against you—there was no way you could prefail."

I nodded, my face a mask of pain and weariness.

Kallian's expression darkened as he recounted the aftermath. "The Persians lingered for most of the day, picking through the dead for trophies. They took their time, laughing and jeering as they stripped the fallen of their armor and valuables. I was impatient, fearful that without my timely intervention, you'd die."

The memory of those agonizing hours was clear in his eyes. He clenched his fists, the frustration of helplessness still raw. “Finally, they left and I got to you as quickly as I could. I was terrified I would find you already gone.”

He paused, the silence between us heavy with unspoken emotions.

“And the rest, you know,” Kallian finished softly.

Nodding, I rested my hand gently on his shoulder and met his eyes before slowly getting to my feet. Instantly, my head began to spin and I felt like I would fall. My body was both weak and still healing from its wounds.

"We need to leave. The Persians will likely be using this pass as a supply route for their army—plus it’s a five-day ride to the chambers of the vrykolakas council.”

“Why are we going there?”

“Firstly, to inform them of what has transpired here. Secondly, to speak with Megareus. Hopefully, he will be able to assist us in our quest to locate Lycurgus."

Kallian looked at me, his eyes sparking with excitement, though tempered by the somberness of the events he had just witnessed. Briefly, the golden light of the setting sun caught in his dark curls, and for a moment, I was struck by his resilience and beauty, even as exhaustion traced lines across his face.

“Yes! I have to know if it’s possible!” he replied, his voice filled with anticipation.

I nodded, feeling a flicker of hope myself. The journey ahead would be perilous, and Lycurgus’ location was uncertain, but the possibility of finding a solution for Kallian made it worth the risk.

We then began to maneuver through the wreckage of shattered spears and broken shields, amidst the bodies of our comrades and foes.

"Do you think there are any other survivors? Should we check the bodies?" Kallian asked, his voice barely above a whisper, strained with pain and fatigue.

I shook my head, the sorrow for our fallen brothers weighing heavily on me. "No, I don't sense any signs of life. At least their sacrifice was not in vain. The main part of Leonidas' army is now more than a day's ride from here. They will live to fight another day!"

Our steps were heavy with grief as we walked, the echoes of the battle haunting our every move. The bravery, final stand, and deaths of our fellow warriors lingered in the air like a dark cloud, a stark reminder of the desperate fight we had waged—a fight we knew was doomed from the start.

Finally, we reached the edge of the battlefield and paused by a small stream. The water came as a welcome relief from the dust and blood that clung to us. Kneeling, we both drank deeply, the cool water washing away some of the day's horrors.

Chapter Thirty-Seven

Kallian

480 BCE

Aristion and Kallian arrived at a small town nestled deep within the Pindus Mountains, a remote part of the rugged and extensive range. The town's gate was an imposing structure, crafted from heavy timber reinforced with iron bands, weathered by time and the elements. It stood as a testament to the town's enduring strength and resilience. Guarding the entrance was a lone sentinel, a man with a weathered face and piercing eyes that scanned the approaching figures with suspicion.

As Aristion and Kallian drew nearer, the guard's eyes widened in recognition. His stern expression softened, and a broad smile spread across his face. "Aristion? Is it truly you?" the guard exclaimed, his voice tinged with disbelief.

"It's been a long time, Nikias," Aristion replied, his own face lighting up with a smile. "Fifteen years, if I'm not mistaken."

Nikias nodded, stepping forward to clasp Aristion's arm in a firm grip. "Too long, my friend. Too long. Welcome back."

As they walked through the gate, the town revealed itself as a place of quiet strength and subtle beauty. The streets were lined with modest stone houses, each built with a blend of functionality and rustic charm. To a casual observer, the town looked like any other isolated mountain settlement. However, Aristion knew better.

"This town is positioned strategically," Aristion began, his voice low as he spoke to Kallian. "Its location provides natural fortification and seclusion, perfect for our needs. From here, it appears normal, but in truth, with few exceptions, the inhabitants are all vrykolakas."

Kallian's eyes widened with surprise.

"The remoteness ensures privacy and secrecy for our training. The Pindus range spans a significant portion of northern Greece, offering strategic vantage points for monitoring movements in the region, including major trade routes and nearby city-states. We can see anyone coming long before they arrive."

He continued, "Additionally, the mountains are rich in natural resources. We have fresh water from mountain streams, wild game to feed our non vrykolakas inhabitants, and materials for crafting weapons and shelter. This location is perfect for the council seat of the vykolakas. It's been in existence for hundreds of years, completely unobserved by humanity."

Kallian looked around, his eyes taking in the details with newfound respect. "It's incredible. A hidden sanctuary in the mountains."

Aristion nodded. "Indeed. The council has thrived here, training and guiding new vrykolakas in seclusion and safety."

They walked through the winding streets, the townsfolk nodding respectfully as they passed. The air was crisp and clean, filled with the scent of pine and the distant murmur of a mountain stream. The sun was beginning to dip below the horizon, casting long shadows across the stone buildings.

Finally, they arrived at a modest stone house. Aristion stepped forward and knocked on the heavy wooden door. The sound echoed through the quiet evening, and moments later, the door creaked open.

A tall figure stood in the doorway, his face partially obscured by the shadows inside. "Aristion," the figure exclaimed, his voice deep and resonant. "Welcome home. It's been way too long!"

Aristion inclined his head in greeting. "Megareus. It's good to see you."

Megareus stepped aside, gesturing for them to enter.

As they entered the house, the warmth and familiarity of the place washed over him. The room smelled of aged wood, with a sense of tranquility permeating the air. The walls were adorned with tapestries depicting ancient battles and serene landscapes, reflecting the rich culture of the vrykolakas.

Megareus, a tall and imposing figure with long gray hair cascading down his back, stood waiting. He wore simple yet sturdy trousers, a leather belt cinched at his waist, and a plain smock that hinted at his practicality and lack of vanity. His eyes indicated both wisdom and strength, hinting at the many centuries he had lived and the countless experiences he had endured.

"Megareus," Aristion said, his voice respectful. "This is Kallian. He's been working with me in Sardis."

Megareus extended a hand, his grip firm and welcoming. "Welcome, Kallian."

Aristion then turned to Megareus, his expression grave. "I must take my leave to meet with the council. I bear news of the Persian invasion. Leonidas is dead. He was defeated at Thermopylae."

Megareus' face fell at the mention of Thermopylae. "Leonidas... defeated?" he whispered, horror etched into his features. "This is grave news indeed."

Aristion nodded, a shadow passing over his face. "I will return once I have spoken with them. Kallian, you are in good hands." With that, he turned briskly and left the house, his footsteps echoing through the quiet streets. The sound grew softer and softer until it faded into the distance, leaving an expectant silence in its wake.

Megareus turned to Kallian, his expression softening. "Come, sit with me. Let's have a drink." He poured two goblets of wine from a clay jug, the rich, dark liquid reflecting the firelight. The aroma of aged grapes filled the room, mingling with the scent of burning wood. Handing one goblet to Kallian, Megareus gestured to a pair of wooden chairs near the hearth. They sat, the warmth of the fire providing a comforting backdrop to their conversation.

Kallian took a sip of the wine, savoring its taste. "I've been working undercover with Aristion for over two years in Sardis," he began. "We had to leave quickly after being discovered and needed to relay the disposition of Xerxes' invasion fleet to Leonidas," sorrow evident in his voice as he uttered the name of the fallen monarch.

Megareus listened intently, his eyes sharp and thoughtful, as Kallian spoke at length about his time in Sardis, discussing the intricacies of their mission, the dangers they faced, and the urgency of their escape. When Kallian paused, the room fell into a contemplative silence, the crackle of the hearth the only sound.

Then, Megareus leaned back, appraising Kallian with a quizzical eye. After a moment, he broke the silence. "Tell me, Kallian, what is your connection with Aristion? Is it merely business, or something more...?" His voice trailed off, leaving the question hanging in the air, as if he were hesitant to voice the final implication.

Kallian looked a bit embarrassed, his cheeks flushing slightly. He nodded, confirming Megareus' suspicions. "Yes, it's more…"

Megareus laughed heartily, slapping Kallian on the back. "It's about time! Aristion has been alone for far too long. I'm happy for you both."

Kallian smiled, feeling a weight lifted off his shoulders. "Thank you—your support means a lot."

As the moment's warmth began to fade, Kallian's expression shifted, growing serious. The lightheartedness left his eyes, replaced by a look of intent focus. He leaned forward slightly, his voice dropping to a more earnest tone. "I have a question, or rather, a favor to ask," he began. "Do you happen to know the whereabouts of Lycurgus?"

Megareus studied Kallian for a moment, his eyes narrowing slightly. "Why do you seek Lycurgus?"

Kallian took a deep breath. "I want Aristion to turn me into a vrykolakas. We believe Lycurgus may hold the key."

Megareus let out a long sigh, nodding in understanding. "Aristion has a long memory. It was many years ago I told him about the rumor surrounding Lycurgus falling in love with a mortal woman. But I must warn you, much of it is hearsay. Lycurgus may not be able to help.

However, Aristion is like a son to me. Even if there's only an outside chance that what I know can assist you, I will offer my assistance willingly."

Kallian's eyes filled with gratitude, a sense of relief washing over him.

"Thank you. That means more than you know," he said, his voice filled with genuine appreciation.

Their conversation continued deep into the night. They discussed the ancient history of the vrykolakas and the challenges of living hidden from humanity. Megareus recounted old legends and battles, his voice rich with the weight of centuries.

The fire in the hearth burned low, casting long shadows on the stone walls, when a brief knock at the door broke the comfortable silence that had settled over the room.

Megareus rose to answer it, his movements fluid and graceful, and was greeted by Aristion, his expression serious.

He immediately gestured for him to sit and appraised him before speaking. "You look weary."

"Yes, having to go into detail about the events of the past few days, although necessary, was not pleasant. I would have preferred not to have had to relive it."

"Understandable, my friend, understandable. I can only imagine how challenging it's been for you both!"

Aristion took a deep breath, and there was a brief moment of silence before he spoke again. "On another subject, has Kallian told you of our desire to locate Lycurgus?"

"Yes, we barely got through the pleasantries before he dropped that one on my lap," Megareus chuckled, then continued. "I know exactly where the old goat is, even though he's gone to great pains to keep it a secret. He does not like visitors and is quite reclusive."

“Well, the council has tasked me to seek his aid, since his knowledge and experience could be crucial in our fight against the Persians. Reclusive or not, if Greece falls, he will have to live with the consequences, most of which are not conducive to his quiet life!”

"Or mine," Megareus replied, sighing. "And then, of course, there's the matter of Kallian's desire to become a vrykolakas. I don’t know if Lycurgus has the answer, but he might. He doesn’t talk about the circumstances under which he met his wife. Most say she was already a vrykolakas, but there is an unsubstantiated rumor that she may have been mortal."

“Even if there’s only a slight chance he can help, it’s worth asking,” Aristion replied, his tone resolute. “Either way, we have to leave at first light. Given the speed at which the Persians are moving, time is of the essence. The council wants Lycurgus here immediately.”

Chapter Thirty-Eight

Aristion

480 BCE

We were mere paces from the door when we were startled by a voice from behind us.

"How can I help you?"

We spun around to face its source. Rising from the brush, a figure cloaked in darkness emerged, his gaze locking onto mine with a piercing intensity. The man looked old, easily in his eighties, with a weathered face etched by the passage of time. Yet, I knew his appearance was deceiving. Lycurgus was a vrykolakas Elder, many hundreds of years old. The way he carried himself spoke of a strength and vitality far younger than his years would suggest. His posture was erect, his movements fluid and deliberate.

The dim light of dusk revealed more details of the enigmatic figure. His face, framed by a mane of silver hair, bore a kindly yet stern expression. Deep lines crisscrossed his skin, each one telling a story of battles fought and wisdom gained. Despite the warmth in his eyes, there was an undeniable menace about him, a keen glint that hinted at depths of knowledge and power. This was Lycurgus, everything I had imagined and more.

"We seek Lycurgus," I replied, my voice steady despite the surprise. "We bring an urgent message from the Council, and also something more private in nature."

Lycurgus stepped closer, his gaze never wavering. "The Council, you say?"

He studied us for a long moment, the silence stretching out uncomfortably, before he finally nodded.

"Very well. Come inside. We will speak further," he said, turning towards the hut.

We followed him, our footsteps crunching softly on the loose stones that covered the ground. Inside, the space was larger than it appeared from the outside. Shelves lined the walls, filled with ancient tomes and peculiar artifacts. A large wooden table occupied the center of the room, its surface cluttered with scrolls, maps, and mysterious vials. The air was thick with the scent of old parchment and a hint of incense.

Lycurgus motioned for us to sit at the table as he settled into a chair opposite us, his piercing eyes scanning our faces.

"Selene," he called out, his voice resonating through the room, "we have guests."

From a back room, a woman entered, moving with a grace that was both commanding and gentle. She appeared to be in her middle years, her beauty striking and timeless. Her dark hair cascaded over her shoulders in loose waves, framing a face that was both serene and captivating. Her eyes, a deep shade of blue, sparkled with intelligence and warmth. High cheekbones and a smooth complexion hinted at her enigmatic nature, much like her husband.

Her attire was simple yet elegant, a flowing dress that accentuated her slender figure. She carried herself with a poise that suggested a strength and resilience matching that of Lycurgus. As she approached, a soft smile touched her lips, though there was a hint of curiosity in her gaze.

"Selene," Lycurgus said, his tone softer now, "this is Aristion and Kallian. They bring a message from the Council."

She nodded in acknowledgment, her eyes flickering between us. "Welcome," she said, her voice melodic and soothing. "Please, make yourselves comfortable. Can I get you something to drink?"

"Thank you," I replied, feeling a sense of ease in her presence. "Yes, that would be welcome."

Selene disappeared momentarily and returned with a tray of goblets filled with a rich, dark liquid. As we sipped the drink, which tasted of spiced wine, Lycurgus turned his attention back to us. "Now, what does that inferno Council want of me?" his tone one of exasperation.

I took a deep breath, gathering my thoughts. "Xerxes has invaded Greece. They are advancing rapidly and the Council believes your insight is crucial to preventing their success. They've requested your immediate help."

Lycurgus's eyes narrowed. "I don't answer to the Council. In fact, I have no desire to involve myself in human affairs," he replied, sounding irritated.

"But if they succeed, it will impact you, surely?" I pressed.

"No, I'll just disappear. There are plenty of places where we can live undisturbed by the trivial matters of mankind. As far as I'm concerned, the matter is closed!" his tone one of finality. "However, I'm curious. What is your more personal request?"

Both Kallian and I glanced at each other nervously. Lycurgus immediately rolled his eyes. "Don't bother, I already know!" he said, letting out a chuckle. "So, Kallian, you want to become a vrykolakas?"

"How... how..." Kallian stuttered, unable to complete the sentence, his expression one of shock.

"Is it that obvious?" I laughed.

Lycurgus leaned back, a smirk playing at the corners of his mouth. "It's written all over your companions face," he replied turning to me.

Kallian's eyes widened, and he nodded vigorously. "Yes! Can you help?" His voice was eager, almost pleading, intermingled with a hint of desperation.

Lycurgus's humor quickly faded, replaced by a slumping of his shoulders and a big sigh. "I guess the rumor regarding Selene has now become public knowledge. I'm going to be inundated with requests. I don't think I'll even wait to see what happens with the Persians. I should disappear immediately!"

Kallian, looking a little perturbed, quickly glanced at me before his gaze settled back on Lycurgus. The direction the conversation was heading was unsettling. Lycurgus then became silent and contemplative before looking Kallian squarely in the eyes, his expression serious.

"Fine. Since you are already here, I am prepared to entertain your request. However, I must tell you, this is a dangerous and irreversible decision. It will change you in ways you cannot imagine. Are you truly prepared for that?"

Kallian swallowed hard, his determination clear. "I am."

"Well, as some have surmised, my wife was human when we met. I turned her."

I couldn't contain my curiosity. "How is that possible? Most humans die during a turning. Why did you take such a chance?"

Lycurgus's eyes bore into mine, a mix of patience and mild reproach.

"Aristion, you are omitting one crucial detail. Unlike you, I am an elder. Elders can turn humans without risk. However, it is something we don't talk about and have seldom done since the 'Great Betrayal'."

An ominous silence descended over the room, the last two words hanging in the air. I knew very little about this topic, and my curiosity was piqued. Tentatively, I broached the subject. "What exactly was the 'Great Betrayal'? It is mentioned in the council records, but there are few details."

"That's because the surviving elders don't like to talk about it," Lycurgus replied. "Suffice it to say, we were created, rather than turned—which you already know!"

Given Lycurgus's obvious reluctance to discuss the topic, I tried to raise a warding hand as I noticed Kallian about to speak, but it was too late.

"What do you mean by created, not turned?" he blurted out, his youth and lack of diplomatic skills getting the better of him.

For a brief, fleeting moment, it looked like Lycurgus was about to snap at Kallian, but then he let out a deep exhale and leaned forward, his eyes dark with the weight of history. "During a huge offensive against the city of Pylos in the time of Heracles, Hades emerged from the Underworld to defend the city. To aid in its defense, he created thirty vrykolakas—the original Elders, including myself. We were meant to be an unstoppable force against Heracles. However, Heracles managed to wound Hades, who, in his weakened state, abandoned us and retreated back to the Underworld, leaving us to fend for ourselves."

The room seemed to darken as Lycurgus continued, "With Hades gone, chaos ensued. We, the Elders, turned many humans into vrykolakas to bolster our numbers, but the newly turned lacked control and succumbed to their bloodlust. Pylos was overrun, and our kind spread terror and destruction, unable to curb our insatiable hunger. It was a very dark age for humanity, and we were at the heart of it."

Lycurgus's expression hardened, his voice filled with bitterness. "We Elders have never forgiven Hades for his betrayal. His abandonment led to untold suffering, and we bore the brunt of the blame. Since then, we have struggled to bring order among our kind, forever marked by the chaos we once unleashed. It is a burden we carry, a reminder of the dark power that created us and the god who forsook us. It is also one of the reasons why we don't share the knowledge about our ability to successfully turn humans into vrykolakas."

He fell silent, and I absorbed the gravity of his words. Casting my eyes around the room, I took in the shelves laden with ancient tomes and scrolls. The weight of history and secrets emanating from the small space was palpable.

"Anyway, enough of the history lesson, let's get back to you!" he said, his tone lightening.

Lycurgus glanced at us quizzically as we exchanged hopeful looks. It must have been obvious to him that we shared an incredibly strong bond and love for each other, much like he did with his wife.

Nodding slowly, he continued. "I understand why you wish to be turned, and it has nothing to do with power," he said softly, the corners of his mouth turning up in a slight smile. "So yes, young human, I will turn you. However, the process is not to be taken lightly. You will be forever changed. Your humanity will become but a distant memory."

Kallian looked down, contemplating for a moment, before meeting Lycurgus's eyes. "I understand," he said finally. "I've considered this for a long time. I'm ready."

Lycurgus sighed, a mix of resignation and acceptance in his eyes. "Very well. We will begin preparations soon. But know this, Kallian: once the transformation starts, there is no turning back."

Selene, who had been quietly observing, stepped forward. "If this is truly your wish, Kallian, you need to understand that the path before you is fraught with challenges. It will take many years of training for you to learn how to control the insatiable thirst for blood that will ensue from the transformation."

Aristion nodded, the relief evident in his voice. "I can help him with that."

Lycurgus rose from his chair, his movements fluid and purposeful. "Then we shall commence with the process tomorrow morning. Tonight, rest and prepare yourself."

As we settled into the evening, I found myself staring into the flickering flames of the hearth, contemplating the events that had brought us here.

Kallian approached me, his face determined yet anxious. "I feel like a huge weight has been lifted from my shoulders—from our shoulders. We can now be together, truly together."

"Yes, Kallian, for life," I said before adding with a chuckle, "Which, thanks to Lycurgus, is now going to be a little longer than expected!"

As the night wore on, we prepared for what was to come, knowing that the nature of our relationship was about to irrevocably change—hopefully for the better. Yet, despite my optimism, I could not shake the lingering uncertainty about Kallian's ability to handle the challenges of becoming a vrykolakas.

Chapter Thirty-Nine

Kallian

480 BCE

Kallian drifted in a strange, disjointed dream. Flashes of memory flickered like erratic lightning in the dark recesses of his mind. A woman's face, soft and tender—a distant echo of lullabies. The scene shifted abruptly to the harsh rigor of the agoge, where he and Eioneus had trained tirelessly. The feel of Eioneus' cheek against his, a fleeting comfort amidst the brutality of their environment. Then, memories flowed to him of his life with Aristion in Sardis—their shared laughter, the gentle touch of hands, and the warmth of a kiss.

Suddenly, his dreams took a darker turn, merging with foreign memories not his own. A savage battle within an ancient city. The sight of bodies strewn across the streets, the air thick with the stench of blood and decay, and the cacophony of screams. He was engulfed by an insatiable hunger, a terrifying and primal need for blood that consumed his very being. He screamed, and then all went dark.

~

A voice penetrated the silence, gentle and familiar. "Kallian... Kallian... come back to me." It cut through the darkness, warm and soothing, pulling him from the depths of unconsciousness, guiding him back towards the light of wakefulness. His eyelids fluttered, heavy and resistant, but gradually they opened.

The first thing he saw was Aristion's face, filled with concern and relief. Their eyes met, and a wave of warmth washed over Kallian, grounding him in the present moment. Aristion smiled softly, his eyes glistening.

"Hello, little one," Aristion whispered, his voice a tender caress. Kallian's lips curved into a faint smile, the familiarity and love in those words anchoring him back to reality.

"Aristion," Kallian murmured, his voice weak but steadying as he focused on the face of the man he loved. The terrifying visions and memories faded into the background, replaced by the comforting presence of Aristion.

"You're safe," Aristion reassured, gently brushing a lock of hair from Kallian's forehead. "I've got you. Everything is going to be alright."

Kallian took a deep breath. No sooner had he done so than he realized something was different. He was different.

He could hear the steady, rhythmic beating of Aristion's heart, each thump resonating like a drum. Subtle sounds from outside the hut reached his ears—the rustling of leaves, the distant murmur of a stream, the gentle whisper of the wind. He even detected the faint heartbeat of a rabbit outside the door, its rapid pulse fluttering in the stillness of the night.

The world around him was alive with sensations he had never experienced before. The scent of the earth, the wood of the hut, and even the faint aroma of flowers in bloom filled his nostrils with vivid intensity. His vision was sharper; even in the dim light of the room, the textures of the worn wooden beams, the intricate patterns in the fabric of the tapestries, and the fine dust particles floating in the air were now all vividly distinct.

Kallian's newfound awareness was overwhelming yet exhilarating. He turned his gaze back to Aristion, seeing him more clearly than ever before. Every line and curve of his face, the slight tremble of his lips, and the depth of his eyes were now strikingly vivid.

"Aristion," Kallian whispered, his voice filled with wonder. "I can hear... everything. I can feel everything."

Aristion nodded, a gentle smile playing on his lips. "Welcome to your new reality, Kallian. You're one of us now."

"How long was I unconscious?" Kallian asked, still marveling at his enhanced senses.

"It's now late afternoon. You've been out since yesterday morning."

Kallian's mind raced. "Where is Lycurgus? And Selene?"

Aristion's grimaced. "They left this morning. They want nothing to do with the conflict. They just want to be left alone. However, their choice has come with a boon. They've given us the use of their home for as long as we want it. You now have a safe place to adjust to your new life."

Kallian nodded, feeling a strange sense of peace wash over him. Despite the intensity of his new senses and the enormity of his transformation, the presence of Aristion made him feel grounded.

They sat for a while, giving Kallian time to climatize. The minutes passed in comfortable silence. Kallian, though overwhelmed by the newness of his senses, found solace in Aristion's presence. Eventually, curiosity and restlessness won over.

"I want to go outside," Kallian said, his voice steady but eager.

Aristion looked apprehensive but nodded. "Alright, but stay close to me."

They ventured out just as the sun was setting, the air cool and crisp. The world outside was a symphony of sensations for Kallian. Every leaf rustling in the breeze, every distant animal call, every scent carried by the wind was magnified. He was in wonder, drinking in the vivid details that surrounded him.

However, there was a strange feeling within him that was growing stronger—a hunger. As soon as he became aware of it, the sensation intensified and began to consume him. He saw a deer in the distance, and he could sense the beating of its heart and the pulsating of the veins in its neck. The desire to feed surged within him, primal and uncontrollable. He began to move towards the deer, his instincts taking over.

Aristion noticed the change and spoke tentatively, "Kallian, are you alright?"

Kallian struggled to find his voice, the hunger overwhelming him. "Aristion... no... help me... I can't control myself... help me."

Aristion moved quickly, grabbing Kallian and forcing him to meet his gaze. "Look at me. You are beginning to feel the hunger. You must feed."

With that, Aristion sliced his arm with the knife at his belt and held the bleeding wound to Kallian's mouth. "Drink."

At that point, Kallian lost all sense of self-control. He latched onto Aristion's arm, his senses exploding with the taste of blood. It was intoxicating, unlike anything he had ever experienced. The rich, metallic flavor flooded his mouth, and he could feel the life force coursing through him. The blood was warm and potent, filling him with a surge of energy and a sense of euphoria. Every swallow intensified the sensation, drowning out all rational thought and leaving only the primal satisfaction of feeding.

Kallian's vision sharpened further, colors becoming more vivid, and his hearing picked up the subtlest of sounds. The world seemed to pulse with a newfound vibrancy.

After what felt like an eternity, Aristion gently pulled his arm away. Kallian, sated and trembling, looked up at him with wide eyes. "I'm sorry," he whispered, the reality of what he had done sinking in.

Aristion smiled softly, his own eyes reflecting understanding. "It's alright, my love. This is a part of your new reality. We will get through this together."

Kallian, a smile playing on his lips, met Aristion's gaze. "Yes," he agreed softly.

Aristion pulled Kallian close, their bodies pressing together as he leaned in for a kiss. The moment their lips met, Kallian felt an electric surge of connection. His heightened senses made every sensation more vivid—the warmth of Aristion's breath, the soft texture of his lips, the subtle taste that was uniquely Aristion.

The kiss was more than just a physical act; it was a melding of their souls, an intimate connection that resonated through Kallian's entire being. He could feel Aristion's heartbeat syncing with his own, their breaths intertwining in a shared rhythm. The world around them seemed to dissolve, leaving only the two of them in a timeless moment of pure, unadulterated unity.

When the kiss finally ended, Kallian opened his eyes to find Aristion's face close to his, their foreheads touching. Aristion smiled, his eyes sparkling with affection and mischief.

"Let's go back inside," Aristion suggested, his voice carrying an undertone that made Kallian's heart quicken.

Kallian nodded, a knowing smirk crossing his features, in anticipation of what was to come. Hand in hand, they turned and made their way back into the hut.

Chapter Forty

Aristion

480 BCE

Inside the hut, the flickering firelight cast shadows that danced across the walls. Kallian's eyes, now filled with an intense, smoldering hunger that went beyond bloodlust, locked onto mine. He pulled me toward him, our bodies colliding with a force that was both tender and powerful—his newfound strength eliciting a smile from me. I would no longer have to hold back for fear of hurting him. The power coursing through him was palpable, a thrilling reminder of the transformation he had undergone.

The moment our lips met, the world outside ceased to exist. There was no past, no future, only the raw, electrifying connection between us. Kallian's hands roamed over my body, exploring every contour with a newfound fervor. I could feel the primal energy in his touch, his grip unyielding yet filled with an unmistakable love.

As we stumbled towards the bed, we tore at our clothes, which fell away—forgotten in the heat of the moment.

The muscle between Kallian's legs was now rock hard, arching skyward from the mass of black curly hair at its base to just above his naval. I grasped it with one hand, feeling the pronounced veins running along its length, pulsating with each beat of his heart.

Entwined around each other, his cool skin contrasted sharply with the heat of his kisses trailing down my neck, igniting a fire within me that burned hotter with each touch. Every sensation was heightened, every breath and heartbeat amplified by our shared vrykolakas nature.

We moved together with a rhythm that was primal and instinctive, our bodies synchronizing in perfect harmony. I turned him, and with one arm around his waist, I used my free hand to push the back of his head down towards the covers of the bed. Now, with a hand on each hip, I placed the tip of my shaft between the cheeks of his well-rounded buttocks and entered him—eliciting a groan of pleasure.

“Yes, yes—harder,” he cried, almost pleading, as he pushed back against my shaft in synchrony with each thrust.

The intensity of our lovemaking was beyond anything I had ever experienced, a fusion of physical and emotional ecstasy that left us both breathless. The strength and speed that had resulted from his transformation only added to the passion. Our movements were a blur of raw, unfiltered desire

Turning him over, I raised his legs over my shoulders and entered him again. His eyes, glowing with an ethereal light, met mine as he whispered my name, his voice a husky growl that sent waves of pleasure coursing through me. I responded with equal fervor, gripping his legs and pulling him closer, and feeling the entire length of my manhood slide into him.

In that moment, we were not just lovers but two halves of a whole, bound together by something ancient and unbreakable. The room was filled with the sounds of our union, a symphony of sighs and whispers, gasps and moans. Every touch, every kiss, was a promise—a vow of eternal love and unyielding devotion.

As the crescendo of our passion built to an overwhelming peak, the speed the speed of my thrusts had become a blur of motion—even to my vrykolakas vision. I then began to feel an intense heat building in my groin, quickly followed by an explosion of light and blinding euphoria. I threw my head back and screamed. Almost in unison, the tip of Kallian’s manhood erupted, eliciting a cry of pleasure from him. Again and again his huge shaft pulsated, leaving a trail of glistening pearls in its wake—spanning the entire length of his lean muscular torso.

Trembling in the aftermath of our exchange, we collapsed into each other's arms, our bodies entwined, the room filled with the soft glow of the dying fire. Kallian's head now rested on my chest, his breathing slowly returning to normal. I stroked his hair, feeling the steady thrum of his heart against my skin. The bond between us was stronger than ever, a connection forged in the fires of his transformation and tempered by our love.

"Aristion," Kallian murmured, his voice a contented sigh. "I've never felt anything like that."

"Neither have I," I replied, my own voice filled with wonder and satisfaction. "We are truly one now, bound together."

He looked up at me, his eyes shining with love and determination. "Aristion, whatever comes next, I need you by my side. Given my uncontrolled thirst for blood earlier, I can't do this without you. I don't ever want to be apart from you."

"Together," I echoed, pulling him closer and kissing his forehead. "Always."

As we lay there, wrapped in each other's arms, I knew that no matter what challenges awaited us, our bond would never be broken. We had found something rare and precious, a love that transcended time and mortality. And in that moment, as the night enveloped us in its embrace, I felt a profound sense of peace and fulfillment, knowing that we would face the future as one.

Epilogue

48 BCE

The evening sky was alive with hues of crimson and gold as Aristion and Kallian stood on a low rise, gazing out over the vast, sprawling plain before them. It was 48 BCE, more than four centuries since their paths had first crossed. Over the years, they had witnessed the rise and fall of empires, the relentless march of progress, and countless transformations—both monumental and subtle—that reshaped the world. Yet, for all the change they had seen, the essence of human nature remained untouched, as unyielding as the mountains themselves.

The air around them was thick with tension, charged with the quiet dread of an impending storm. Below, legions of soldiers maneuvered with disciplined precision, arranging themselves into the rigid lines of Caesar and Pompey's armies. Standards bearing the proud symbols of Rome fluttered defiantly in the evening breeze, while the setting sun cast a fiery glow over shields and swords, reflecting off the armor of thousands like scattered stars. Distant shouts of command punctuated the rhythmic clatter of steel, creating a haunting symphony—a grim prelude to the violence about to unfold.

As the clash of battle echoed across the plain, the sun dipped below the horizon, casting long, foreboding shadows over the chaotic scene. Fires burned in the distance, their flickering light illuminating the faces of soldiers locked in mortal combat. The acrid scent of blood and smoke thickened the air, a harsh reminder of the steep price of power and ambition.

Aristion and Kallian stood as silent witnesses to the carnage, their faces etched with a mixture of sorrow and resignation. They had seen this too many times—the inevitable toll exacted by human rulers driven by the thirst for power.

Eventually, the clash of swords quieted, replaced by the groans of the wounded. The battlefield lay littered with broken standards and discarded shields, symbols of Pompey's once-proud army now trampled into the blood-soaked earth—marking the bitter end of a struggle and the triumph of Caesar's will.

In silence, Aristion and Kallian turned away, their silhouettes merging with the encroaching night. Together, they walked into the uncertainty of the future, their steps heavy with the wisdom of hard-won experience. Yet, they carried with them a fragile hope—that perhaps one day, the echoes of war would finally fade, replaced by the quiet harmony of a world at peace.

Made in the USA
Las Vegas, NV
23 December 2024